SAVAGE BITCH

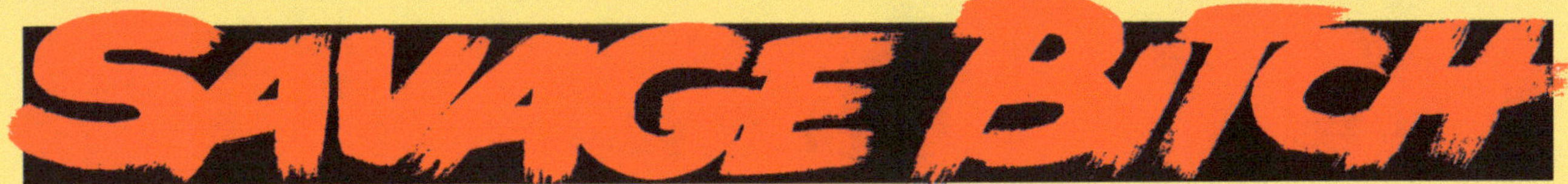

Welcome to this special presentation of ***SAVAGE BITCH***. This is a complete collection of SAVAGE BITCH by **SCAR** – **Steve Carter** and **Antoinette Rydyr**, Australia's foremost and legendary horror sci-fi comic book creators who have been active in the industry for over twenty years.

SAVAGE BITCH was originally published in serialised form in *Picture Magazine* by Australian Consolidated Press (ACP) between 1995 and 1997, as a 'Jungle Girls' adventure like no other; controversial, challenging and bizarre!

I first discovered Steve's work in ***Phantastique*** circa 1986, before later meeting him at OzCon Sydney in 1992. By that time, Steve had met Antoinette in 1991, and together formed the creative team known as S.C.A.R – an acronym of their initials.

I immediately became a fan of their unique style and have been following their career ever since. During the 1990s, we often appeared in the same local comics and magazines – such as Picture. It's been an honour and a privilege to help out my old friends with putting together this complete epic today.

Their wild imagination, unique style and consistent pushing of the boundaries have resulted in the creation of some of the most incredible stories and art that I have seen.

SAVAGE BITCH is an excellent showcase of all of the elements that SCAR are famous for: feisty Amazons, fascinating alien worlds and freakish monsters.

You can see more of their work at www.weirdwildart.com.

– DAVE HEINRICH

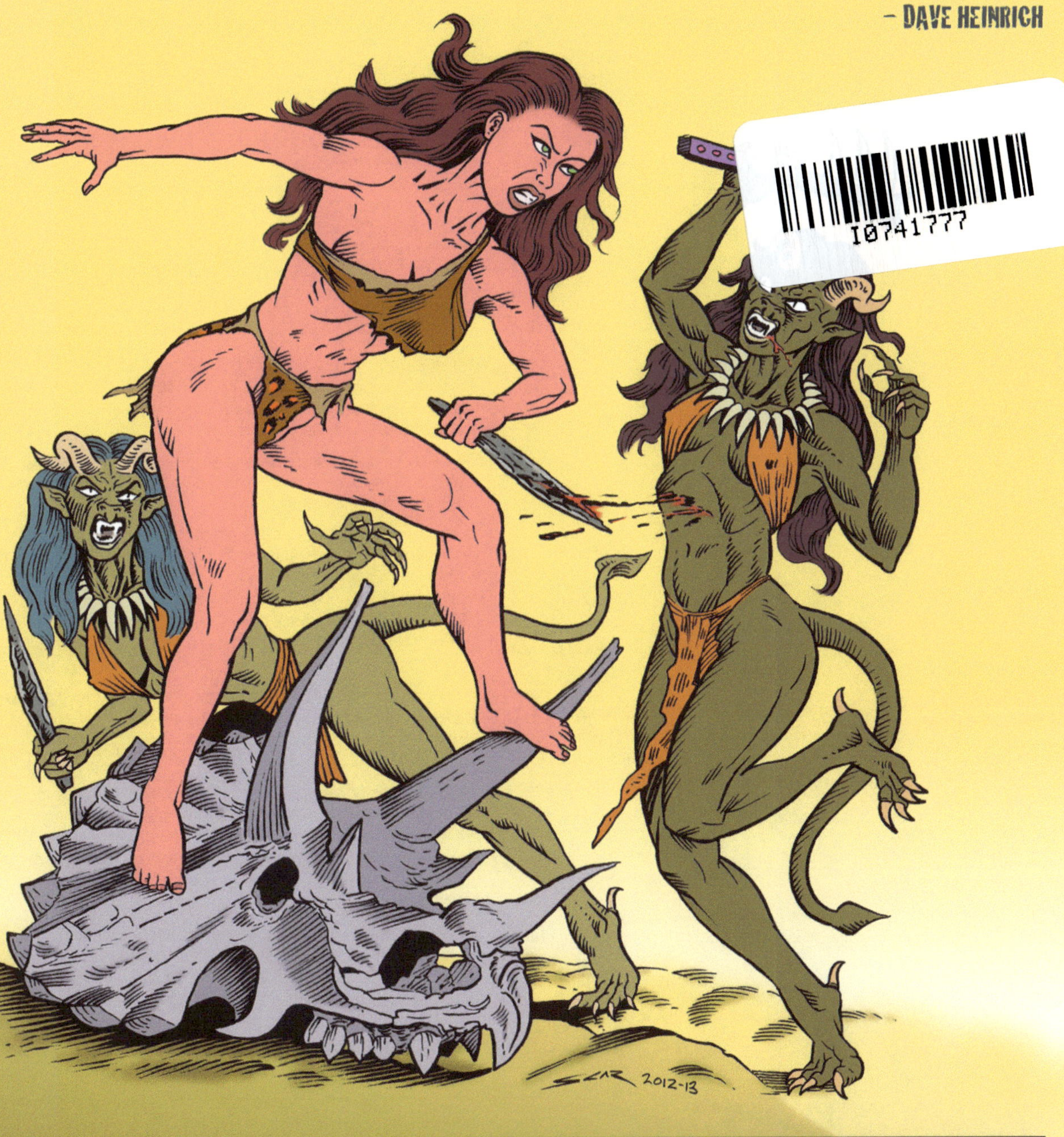

First edition, first printing: November 2013. This SAVAGE BITCH collection is published by SCAR. Designed by Dave Heinrich.

SCARRED FOR LIFE:

NOTES TOWARD A FIELD GUIDE TO S[TEVE] C[ARTER AND] A[NTOINETTE] R[YDYR]

There is an alternate universe – an alternate publishing universe, containing massive bound volumes currently found only in Lucien's Library of Dreams (see Neil Gaiman et al's *Sandman*) – in which I frequently find marvelous paperback field guides to biologies and zoologies and botanies impossible in my day-to-day real world.

Here, in this "real world" universe, the real-world pocket-sized Field Guides of my real-world pocket-sized youth were all written by (or at least supervised by) Herbert S. Zim, and illustrated by a painfully, lovingly over-familiar procession of Western Publishing/Whitman/ Golden Books artists.

The alternate publishing universe field guides are a bit like those – but more like the *Oxford Venomous Creatures of Australia*, Fifth Edition – except for one thing.

The field guides of this alternate universe are predominantly the work of **SCAR**, aka **Steve Carter** and **Antoinette Rydyr**.

These alternate universe field guides are alluring, beautiful, terrifying, and mesmerizing beyond all comprehension. I am both drawn to them and repulsed by/from them; I look, but I cannot look. So, then – I must look.

They are the hidden worlds of what really lives under rocks; what the rocks really are (where rocks have jaws and claws and sexual organs); what really feeds on its own mates and young; what really devours as it rapes; what really slinks through the underbrush and screams in the Outback; what truly has teeth longer than our fingers, talons sharper than our wits, bellies more bloated than any corporation's coffers. They live in realms where the entire world is an externalized intestinal tract, mobilized appetites that can never be sated, where heads are comprised of maws/orbs/genitals that can see/fuck/consume all living things in the same, singular ravenous act.

An "Alien Eden," if you will.

These alternate universe field guides are forbidden and essential, like all truly taboo literature. These field/filed guides are keenly observational, with every detail seen precisely rendered – and intensely imaginative works, giving form to terrible tulpas manifest from reptilian brains.

These alternate universe field guides are everywhere, and nowhere; known, and unknown.

I have read them devotedly since the late 1980s, when I first laid eyes on them. I have horded them since the 1990s, when they began to materialize in our shared known world, artifacts of suspect publishing schemes and debris from discarded wet dreams. I have studied them since the Millennial shift, anticipating their necessity after the Fall of All.

I have dreamed these alternate publishing universe field guides in overlapping dreams with S[teve] C[arter and] A[ntoinette] R[ydyr] (hereafter, per their own moniker synthesis, SCAR, evidence of no gender bias or preference on my part, please and thank you).

Some of those field guides are secreted in that more-real-than-real alternative universe; I cannot share or show them to you.

Some of those field guides are "real-world" real, and you now hold one of them in your hands.

Yes, **Savage Bitch** is a field guide. A graphic novel, to be sure, but a field guide, too.

Quickly – bury or burn it, lest you be SCARred.

Or, join me.

Your choice.

I've obviously made my choice – and here we are.

There is an alternative publishing universe where SCAR never met – that is, SC [Steve Carter] and AR [Antoinette Rydyr] never met.

There are remnants, in this "real world" universe, of what might-have-been. We can chart that alternative reality via "real world" print droppings.

Look, here's some inky scat now:

Here in the "real world" is *Phantastique*, circa 1985-86, a government-grant-and-loan-funded quartet of zines that sought to rupture our known universe with the first eruptions from Carter's internalized/ externalized universe, working with confederates-in-crime like Des Waterman. Here we find published artwork by SC [Steve Carter] slinging ink on his lonesome and signing "**Carnage**."

Working in a drawing style evocative of that ill-fated American underground comix creator Jim Osborne (see *D.O.A.*, 1976; also see Patrick Rosenkranz's article/obit on Osborne in *The Comics Journal*, #242, April 2002) – hard delineation of organic forms, rendered with crystalline clarity and a perfectly sterile, crisp line – SC embodied and transcended his self-proclaimed influences (pulp sf, underground comix, etc.).

SC aka Carnage's work immediately infuriating the Aussie Left – what Carter himself later referred to as "an unholy union of feminist and fundamentalists" – which attacked Phantastique as an assaultive work and an abomination all the more reprehensible for having been government-funded. Thus, SC found himself in the stellar subversive company of **David Cronenberg** right out of the starting gate. Cronenberg's instructional cinematic field guide to a peculiar Canadian strain of genetically-spawned invasive phallic/fecal sexual parasite, released as Shivers around the world in 1976 (and in America as They Came From Within), had also been in part government-funded.

Unlike Phantastique, Cronenberg's Shivers spilled as much money as it did semen-stained stage blood into Canadian hands, so Cronenberg's transgression ultimately earned more government tax shelter funding and launched careers and the rest is history.

Only in the alternative publishing universe did Phantastique's similar artistic atrocities launch similar international media careers. Those career arcs exist only in Lucien's Dream Library.

Here, in our mundane not-dream "real world," SC was thereafter a marked man. SC's infamy was a stigmata: a scar (not yet SCAR) to be worn with pride, for sure, but a wound, nonetheless. But that which does not exsanguinate us quickly and completely only makes us louder, madder, and more vicious. As always, the forces of repression – briefly victorious in their quashing of Phantastique – only bred fresh abominations from SC's lair.

In comix, a marked man only makes more marks. Proving anew that artists are like cockroaches and other verminous lifeforms, the life equation to be committed to memory is "repression = more urgent expression," ad infinitum.

Artists are also not only capable of, but immediately shift into, spontaneous self-procreation under such conditions. At this point still capable only of self-reproduction, marsupial mutant SC fucked himself and toted around his offspring like a maternal arachnid or puff-cheeked Cardinalfish (the males harbor their broods in their mouths), depositing his Carnage-Joeys where ever he found fertile ground.

I have in my hands now the first issues of *Terror Australis*: The Australian Horror and Fantasy Magazine, printed in the late 1980s in quantities of only 500 in Sydney South, New South Wales, by one **Leigh Blackmore**. Here we find more published artwork by SC, illustrating stories by **Maurice Xanthos** and reviews of then-current 1988 genre literature, including horror and fantasy magazines and fanzines. Look, here: an angry tentacled SC cephalopod playing guitar: that about sums it up.

I suspect there are other vaguely-remembered or forgotten lairs hiding more early Carnage creatures.

Any horror harbor in a shitstorm, I always say.

A n aside: In the alternative publishing universe where SCAR never met and SC bore his scars alone, a visionary American writer/artist/ packager/publisher named **Stephen R. Bissette** responded more favorably to his first exposure to SC and published his work in *Taboo*, the short-lived ten-volume (1988-1993) internationally-distributed/ internationally-reviled comics anthology.

In this alternative universe, instead of facing customs busts separately, SRB and SC were busted together, in the same title: Taboo was indeed taboo in many countries, including New Zealand (where we received our most favorable and thorough review ever, and were ultimately allowed to enter their borders as an adults-only publication).

But, in the real-"real-world," SRB was indeed stupid and pig-blind, and did not publish SC's work in Taboo, and missed working with SC at this phase of their separated-by-oceans-and-continents careers.

Stupid, stupid Bissette creature.

Then again, had SRB published SC, would SCAR have ever come together?

Perhaps.

Perhaps not.

Perhaps they may have met sooner.

Perhaps not.

Briefly consulting the I Ching (as he had in 1989), SRB reaffirms that he is blameless.

The Foreword can continue.

End of aside.

I n the "real world," SC/Carnage licked/polished his stigmata clean, as any wounded animal would. He plunged anew into self-packaging/ publishing Charnel House (1991, reissued 1993), a far more aggressive assaultive eye-candy/mindfuck than Phantastique that raised nary a nod from the same forces that had crushed the earlier publication. Charnel House enjoyed coast-to-coast newsstand distribution and made a profit.

This arguably acted as a natural male display of SC's true colors: art functioning like some outsized dewlap or colorful bladder, a tanuki inflating his testicles, SC strutting his fertility and masculinity in a monstrous continental-wide comix rutting dance of cataclysmic proportions.

Proving himself a writing/drawing/editing/publishing marvel, SC found companionship and an artistic mate with which to sire even fiercer monsters.

And oh, what monsters they spawned.

I n this "real world" universe, AR (Antoinette Rydyr) was already making monsters, and found in SC a suitable partner in genetic and artistic crime. She had her own maps and inner compasses, but they met at a comics artists and writers powwow in Sydney in 1991, and, in their own words,

" discovered that we had very common artistic tastes and interests... able to do more together than either of us ever could have achieved on an individual basis..."
SCAR interviewed by James Andre, *Pikitia Press*, Monday, July 9, 2012, http://pikitiapress.blogspot.com/2012/07/steve-carter-and-antoinette-rydyr.html.

AR found in SC a like-minded cartographer of inner scapes and throbbing lifeforms only they could sire.

In a steady stream of drawings, stories (prose and comics form), music (hear their bands: **FistFunk Futurists**, **TeknoSadisT**), screenplays and more, AR and SC found boundless fecundity in their union in every and all media within reach.

They became SCAR and they become Carter Rydyr and they become relentless in their creative pursuits.

I n the alternative publishing universe, SC and AR began creating the field guides to which I referred in the opening paragraph. These monstrous field guides were essential to survival for one and all and kept in eternal print, shelved and available at all times in all bookstores from the hinterlands of New Zealand and Tasmania to the deepest jungles of Papua New Guinea, from Melbourne and Sydney to Darwin and Kakadu and Broome and all points east and west.

In the alternative publishing universe, the SCAR field guides spread like SARS, infecting the globe.

There are SCAR boutique shops and shopping malls in Asia, and Creationist SCAR amusement parks in North America, explaining how male Eden monsters properly subjugate female beings into patriarchal rule and subservience, submitting to the male will.

I n the "real world" publishing universe, fuck that. In this "real world" universe, there are no such field guides, and we must ferret out their monsters and marvels in subterranean places.

In this "real world" universe, SCAR embodies an answer and retort to genre gender "norms" by creating and exploring predatory female archetypes.
"When it comes to art, fiction and fantasy,"
SCAR point out,
" we are both interested in and inspired by the concept and images of hyper-predatory females. Global legend and mythology is full of female monsters and demonic goddesses of destruction
– Lilith, Hecate, Kali, Echidna, Tiamat, Medusa, harpies, banshees, lamiae, etc. These powerful female archetypes have endured throughout history. They provide a diverse source of inspiration for storylines, concepts and characters. There is a plethora of subtext and themes—social, political and Freudian just waiting to be explored through these archetypes..."
(SCAR interviewed by James Andre, Ibid.)

In another interview, excerpted on their website, SCAR noted,

" Our comics are very 'politically correct.' Many of our female characters have assertive roles and 50% of our content is created by a woman and 50% by a man... But seriously, it's hard to have respect for an ideology like political correctness as it is diametrically opposed to free speech..."

Take that, Phantastique-banning feminazis! These vagina dentata bite.

But in this "real world," this took time, and venues, to delineate, articulate, and get down in print. There was a story in Tim Tyler's *Cadaver* #0 (1992), "Carnivore" in *Southern Aurora Comics* (1992), and a censored-by-the-publisher (slapping oversized sound effects over the mayhem to lessen the gore quotient) "**A Mission from God**" in *Slash* #5 and *Splatter* #8 (1993) – yes, too gory for a comic entitled Slash and another entitled Splatter, you read that correctly – the eight-pager "**Half-Caste**" in *Dark Horse Down Under* #3 (1994).

Then they discovered *Fantagraphics*, and Fantagraphics discovered SCAR.

I n the alternative publishing universe, Fantagraphics Books publishers **Gary Groth** and **Kim Thompson** recognized in SCAR the ideal single fusion point for their new imprints, *Monster Comix* and *Eros Comix*. This was recognized immediately in 1991-92, moments after AR and SC met. It was a match made in alternative publishing universe heaven. Thus was launched an ideal synthesis of the initial raw potential.

In this alternative universe, Monster Comics and Eros Comics became one – *Eros Monster* (always put the sex first) – and under a single banner brought together the pop culture monster-movie obsessions of cartoonists like **Gary Panter** (who, after all, had cast ヘドラ/ Hedora as Jimbo's girlfriend) and **Charles Burns** (who, after all, spun his first horror comix from the raw libido of *The Brain That Wouldn't Die*) and novelists like **Tom DeHaven** (who, after all, wrote the seminal monster noir *Freaks' Amour*).

This visionary move brought new comix by these talents into alignment with new work by SCAR, mounting a formidable pop cultural groundswell, sweeping the subcultural aquafirs with alarming new species of comics/comix in a line of comix that continues to be published to this day.

These comix fill an entire shelving unit in Lucien's Dream Library.

A las, in this "real-world" universe, Gary Groth's disdain for genre and contempt for the horror genre in particular colored and curtailed the possibilities. Gary revealed this to me personally in his overture phone call to me in 1991, asking me to do covers (or comix) for the new Monster Comix line.

Like Dr. Frankenstein, Groth admitted nothing but revulsion at any consideration for or contemplation of his own offspring – he spoke disparagingly of the planned Eros line, but held specific self-loathing for the planned Monster Comics, which he never saw as more than an exploitative cash cow to subsidize more highbrow pursuits.

The phone line went dead for a full minute after I suggested he abandon a planned *Attack of the 50-Foot Woman* adaptation (appealing to him solely because Dave Stevens would do covers) to instead get Charles Burns on The Brain That Wouldn't Die. Gary repeated that title back to me slowly, every word dripping with abhorrence; he'd never heard of it, and it was obvious to me he just didn't get it.

The publisher despised the very genre he was seeking to exploit. It was a doomed venture. The results were stillborn at best, yielding only one monsterpiece (Don Simpson's censored King Kong, 1991-92) out of 13 titles to see print in that short-lived two year experiment.

Oh, what might have been!

But we had and have the what-was, and that was sufficient, at the time.

Fantagraphics considered the erotic sf/fantasy cocreations of SCAR as most suitable to the Eros Line, and thus were born/published *Femosaur World* (1993) and their even-more-explicit successors, *Spore Whores* (1994-96) and *Kill of the Spyderwoman* (1995).

I defy you to find any substantial critical assessment of these comix, anywhere. They were strange, repugnant, venomous sex comix, populated by rapacious monsters; they were ugly, assaultive, original, wolfish, and brilliant.

Spore Whores and Kill of the Spyderwoman took place in their own self-contained invented ecosystems. Read 'em and weep.

Femosaur World, however, initiated and was set in what SCAR refer to as "the Alien Eden universe," which includes Planet Nemesis—they've created/published Alien Eden comix zines—and Antoinette tells me that she and Steve "have a ton of stories set in that universe, enough for one or two graphic novels at least... we've also written prose fiction stories set in that world..."– all of which I eagerly await.

Wait no more, though, for the latest Alien Eden saga, Savage Bitch.

You – we – now have it.

In the "real world" we live in, tenacity, fearlessness, and fecundity are virtues. SCAR outlived their coupling with the Eros Comix line, and never looked back. SCAR are into their third decade of creating stories, art, monsters, music, and all manner of media together. SCAR have dealt with more censorship issues (including Australian Customs impounding, initially, their comp copies of their own Eros titles; Spore Whores were subsequently banned from sale).

They never stopped breeding/seeding comix. They continued to contribute to weekly magazines, to comix zines and anthologies – *Blackguard, Decay, The Magazine of Bizarro Fiction*, etc. – and their own publications. Fantastique (government funded and in full color!), *Monstruum*, and *Femonsters* and others followed and/or continue.

Though they are not "a company," SCAR has built its own cottage publishing empire (don't believe me: visit http://www.weirdwildart. com/books/bookchart.html).

Savage Bitch – the book in your mitts – is the first SCAR genuine graphic novel, set (as I just mentioned) in the Alien Eden universe.

You need no prior familiarity with Femosaur World, the Alien Eden comix, or anything else – tuck in, as they say. Approach with caution, though; as with any virgin exploration, the uninitiated may find some nasty surprises and suffer an accident or two. If only we could access that copy of SCAR's Oxford Venomous Creatures of Alien Eden, Sixth Edition in Lucien's Dream Library, we could spare some of you that pain.

Until we get those SCAR-authored-and-illustrated field guides, this will have to do.

For now.

I could go on – articulating the particulars of Alien Eden, its flora and fauna, straining to sculpt in words what SCAR bring to vivid life on the page with pen, brush, ink, and digital tools – but what's the point? You're either with us, or against us; you either dig SCAR, or fled before your eyes kissed the first sentence of this foreword.

Foreword is forearmed.

In those alternative universes I describe, SCAR rule.

In the pages that follow, in this shared universe, SCAR rule, too.

Quickly – bury or burn it, lest you be SCARred.

Or, join me.

Your choice –

I've made mine.

I couldn't be happier to be here.

STEPHEN R. BISSETTE
Mountains of Madness, VT; August 2013

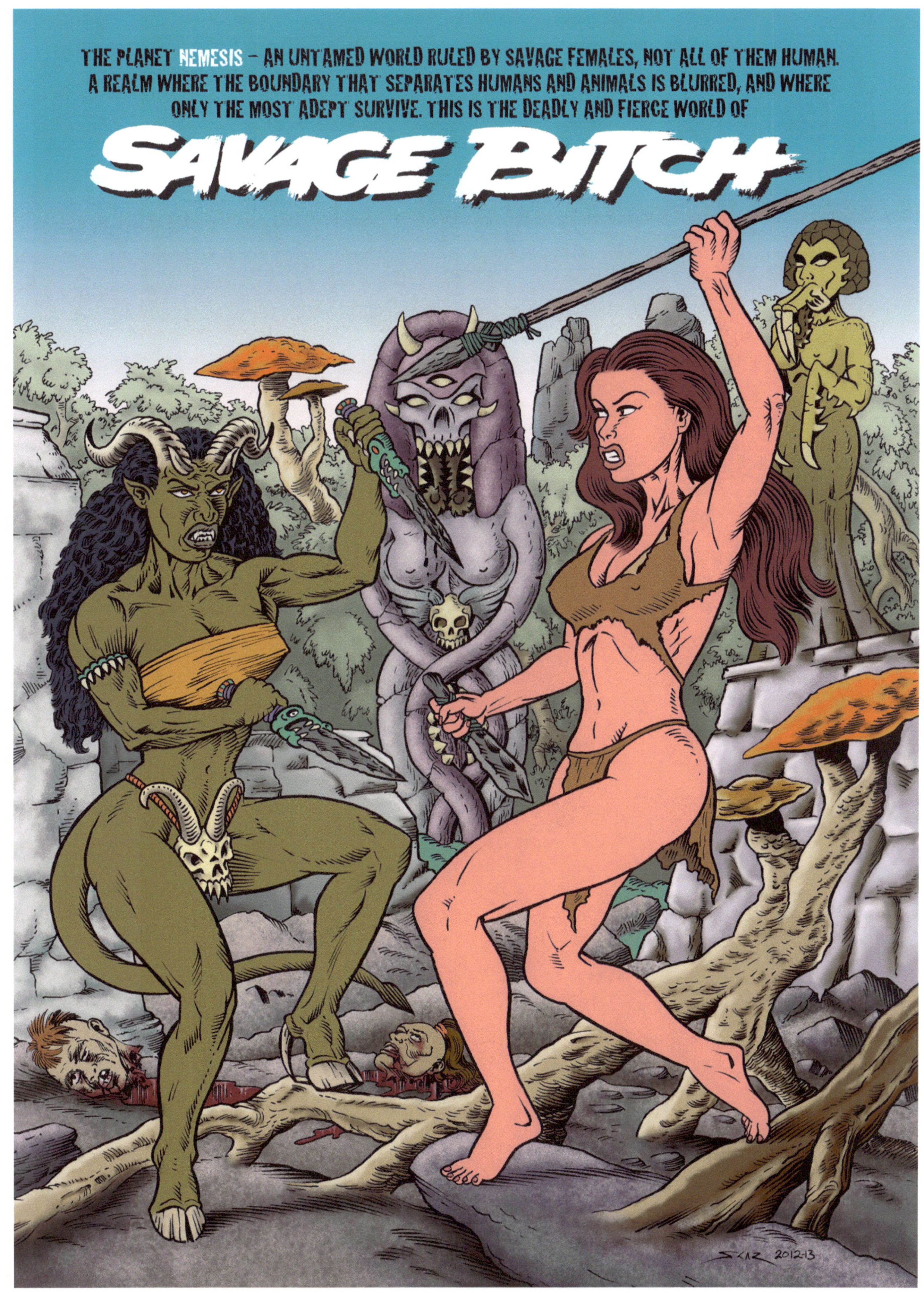

THE PLANET NEMESIS – AN UNTAMED WORLD RULED BY SAVAGE FEMALES, NOT ALL OF THEM HUMAN. A REALM WHERE THE BOUNDARY THAT SEPARATES HUMANS AND ANIMALS IS BLURRED, AND WHERE ONLY THE MOST ADEPT SURVIVE. THIS IS THE DEADLY AND FIERCE WORLD OF
SAVAGE BITCH
SKAZ 2012-13

SAVAGE BITCH
IN THE LAND OF THE
BUKU BUKU
PART ONE
SCAZ
2008

IT'S TIME I HAD A TURN WITH THE MAN...
HA! YOU'RE NOT OLD ENOUGH, YET. YOU'RE STILL A LITTLE SQUIB, SUCKLING AT YOUR MOTHER'S BREASTS!
...IN THE VAST, ALIEN WILDERNESS OF THE MONDO CONGO ON THE STRANGE PLANET NEMESIS, MEN ARE A RARE COMMODITY AND AVAILABLE ONLY TO A PRIVILEGED FEW...
MAYBE YOU'RE GETTING TOO OLD AND IT'S TIME YOU MOVED OVER, YOU OLD CARRION HAG!
YOU WANT THE MAN SO BAD, THEN YOU HAVE TO EARN THE PRIVILEGE AND FIGHT FOR IT LIKE A TRUE HUNTRESS!
LITTLE BITCH'S FAST BECOMING A BRAVE HUNTRESS!
MIGHT DO AT THAT, WILD BITCH, BUT SHE'S NO MATCH FOR BIG BITCH!
KRAK
S. CARTER + A. RYDER ©'95
...HE'S YOURS! AND NOW, INSTEAD OF LITTLE BITCH, YOU'LL BE KNOWN AS SAVAGE BITCH!
MEAT'S GOOD, BUILDS YOUR STRENGTH!
...MEAT STRENGTHENS THE BODY BUT A GIRL ALSO HAS TO FEED HER EMERGING AND HUNGRY SPIRIT ~ AND FOR THAT SHE NEEDS A MAN!

AMONG THE HUMAN TRIBES OF THE MONDO CONGO IT IS THE WOMEN WHO DO THE HUNTING.
CRAZY BITCH, YOU TAKE HARD BITCH AND SNEAK BEHIND THOSE HOPPERS.
BE SURE YOU MAKE THEM RUN BACK THIS WAY.
GOOD! WE'RE UP-WIND...
THEY WON'T KNOW WE'RE HERE UNTIL THEY RUN INTO US. YOU STAY BACK, LITTLE BITCH, BE QUIET AND OBSERVE. LEARN HOW IT'S DONE. ...TRY TO SPEAR ONE IF THEY GET PAST ME.
MY NAME'S SAVAGE BITCH NOW, OR DON'T YOU REMEMBER?! YOU'RE THE ONE WHO GAVE ME THE NEW NAME!
S. CARTER © '95
HERE THEY COME...
...SPEARS READY...
WE'LL EAT WELL TONIGHT!
LITTLE BITCH, YOU'LL HAVE TO CARRY OUR CATCH, SINCE WE HAVE NO MAN WITH US...
THIS IS A MAN'S JOB!
BUT BECAUSE WE ONLY HAVE ONE MAN, AND NO ONE WANTS TO PUT HIM AT RISK OUT HERE, I'VE GOT TO DO IT!
ROTTEN, LAZY MULE THAT HE IS, GETS OUT OF TOO MUCH WORK!
GET OVER HERE, LAZY BRUTE! AND PREPARE THIS CARCASS FOR FEASTING! AND YOU'D BETTER HAVE SWEPT THIS DEN NICE AND CLEAN LIKE I TOLD YOU TO, TOO!
IF IT WEREN'T FOR THE RUTTING I'D BE OUT OF HERE REAL FAST!

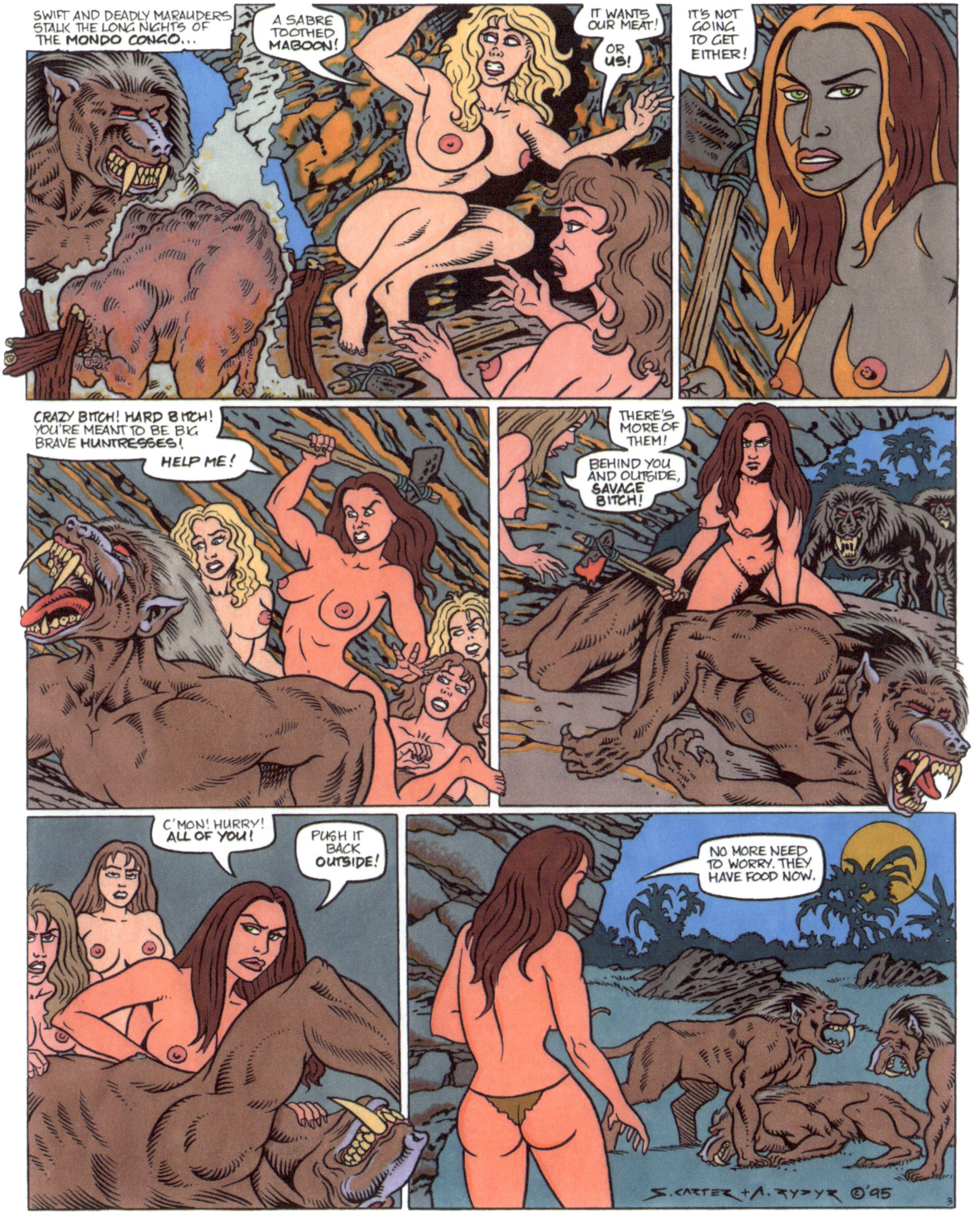

SWIFT AND DEADLY MARAUDERS STALK THE LONG NIGHTS OF THE MONDO CONGO...
A SABRE TOOTHED MABOON!
IT WANTS OUR MEAT! OR US!
IT'S NOT GOING TO GET EITHER!

CRAZY BITCH! HARD BITCH! YOU'RE MEANT TO BE BIG BRAVE HUNTRESSES!
HELP ME!
THERE'S MORE OF THEM!
BEHIND YOU AND OUTSIDE, SAVAGE BITCH!

C'MON! HURRY! ALL OF YOU!
PUSH IT BACK OUTSIDE!
NO MORE NEED TO WORRY. THEY HAVE FOOD NOW.
S. CARTER + A. RYDYR © '95

THIS TIME I DON'T EVEN GET TO GO OUT ON THE HUNT! I'VE GOT TO WATCH OVER THESE FAT MOTHERS AND SEE THAT THE MAN DOES HIS CHORES...
NEVER MIND THE CHORES AND BIG BITCH'S WRATH,
I'VE GOT A BETTER CHORE FOR YOU TO DO RIGHT HERE!
?!
BIG BITCH IS NOT GOING TO BE PLEASED ABOUT THIS...
GET OUT, YOU FAT SOW! AND GET BACK TO NURSING THE YOUNG! YOU'VE GOT NO BUSINESS HERE...!!
...SHE'S DONE NOTHING BUT USE THE MAN ALL DAY! NO WORK HAS BEEN DONE AT ALL!
YOU WERE TOLD TO ATTEND TO THE MOTHERS AND SEE THAT WORK WAS DONE!
ALSO, I DON'T TAKE LIGHTLY TO ANY- ONE WHO TREATS A MOTHER WITH DISRESPECT! NEVER FORGET, THEY WERE ONCE WARRIORS, AND THEY PROTECTED YOU WHEN YOU WERE ONLY THE SIZE OF A TOADLING!
"PERHAPS THE TASK OF BUTCHERING TODAY'S CATCH WILL TEACH YOU A LITTLE RESPECT!"
THIS IS NOT REALLY A GRUNTLING, IT'S ONE OF THOSE FAT MOTHERS!
A. ZYPYR ©'95 S. CARTER

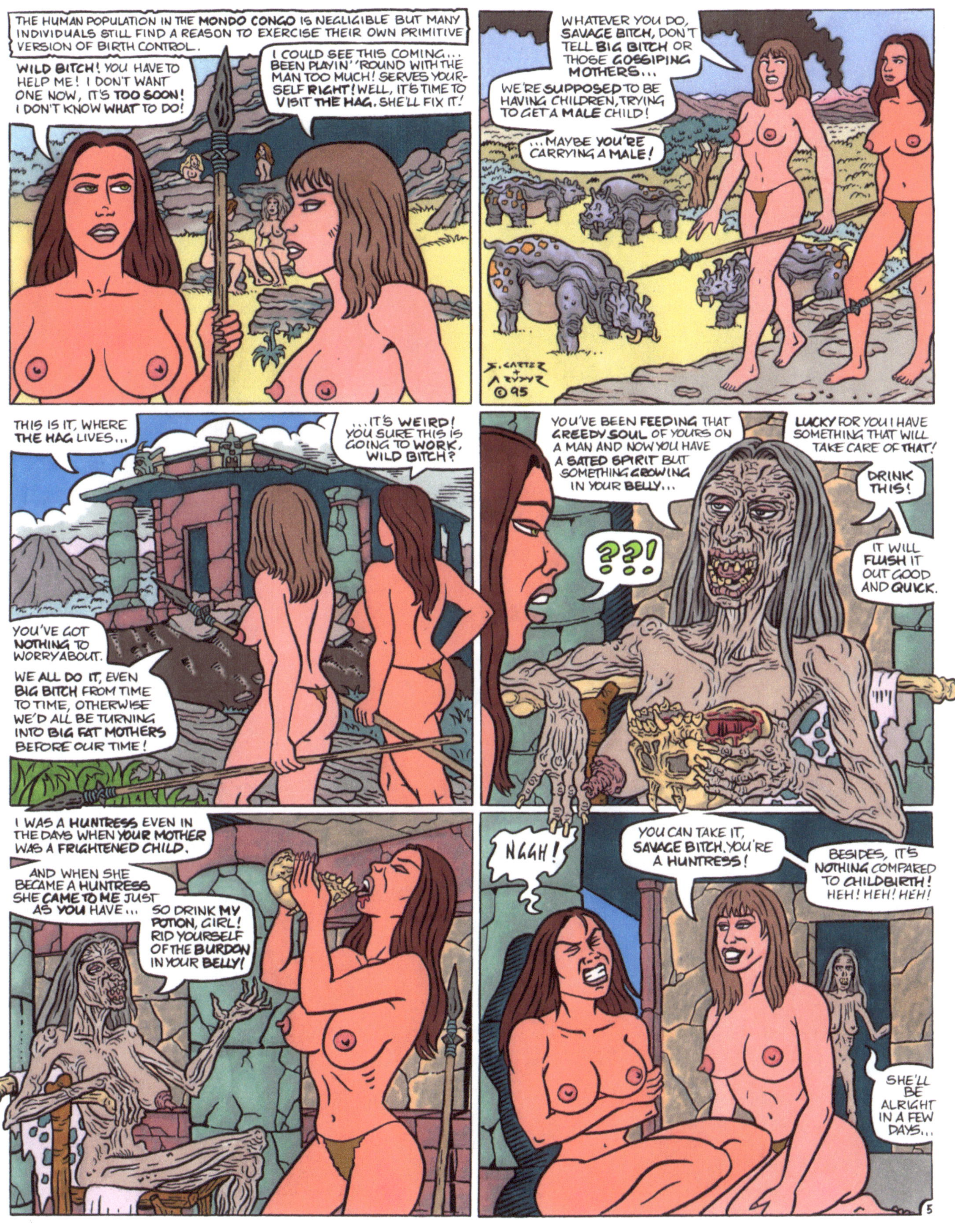

THE HUMAN POPULATION IN THE MONDO CONGO IS NEGLIGIBLE BUT MANY INDIVIDUALS STILL FIND A REASON TO EXERCISE THEIR OWN PRIMITIVE VERSION OF BIRTH CONTROL.
WILD BITCH! YOU HAVE TO HELP ME! I DON'T WANT ONE NOW, IT'S TOO SOON! I DON'T KNOW WHAT TO DO!
I COULD SEE THIS COMING... BEEN PLAYIN' 'ROUND WITH THE MAN TOO MUCH! SERVES YOURSELF RIGHT! WELL, IT'S TIME TO VISIT THE HAG. SHE'LL FIX IT!
WHATEVER YOU DO, SAVAGE BITCH, DON'T TELL BIG BITCH OR THOSE GOSSIPING MOTHERS...
WE'RE SUPPOSED TO BE HAVING CHILDREN, TRYING TO GET A MALE CHILD!
...MAYBE YOU'RE CARRYING A MALE!
S. CARTER + RYDYR © 95
THIS IS IT, WHERE THE HAG LIVES...
...IT'S WEIRD! YOU SURE THIS IS GOING TO WORK, WILD BITCH?
YOU'VE GOT NOTHING TO WORRY ABOUT.
WE ALL DO IT, EVEN BIG BITCH FROM TIME TO TIME, OTHERWISE WE'D ALL BE TURNING INTO BIG FAT MOTHERS BEFORE OUR TIME!
YOU'VE BEEN FEEDING THAT GREEDY SOUL OF YOURS ON A MAN AND NOW YOU HAVE A SATED SPIRIT BUT SOMETHING GROWING IN YOUR BELLY...
LUCKY FOR YOU I HAVE SOMETHING THAT WILL TAKE CARE OF THAT!
DRINK THIS!
??! ...
IT WILL FLUSH IT OUT GOOD AND QUICK.
I WAS A HUNTRESS EVEN IN THE DAYS WHEN YOUR MOTHER WAS A FRIGHTENED CHILD.
AND WHEN SHE BECAME A HUNTRESS SHE CAME TO ME JUST AS YOU HAVE...
SO DRINK MY POTION, GIRL! RID YOURSELF OF THE BURDON IN YOUR BELLY!
NGGH!
YOU CAN TAKE IT, SAVAGE BITCH. YOU'RE A HUNTRESS!
BESIDES, IT'S NOTHING COMPARED TO CHILDBIRTH! HEH! HEH! HEH!
SHE'LL BE ALRIGHT IN A FEW DAYS...
5

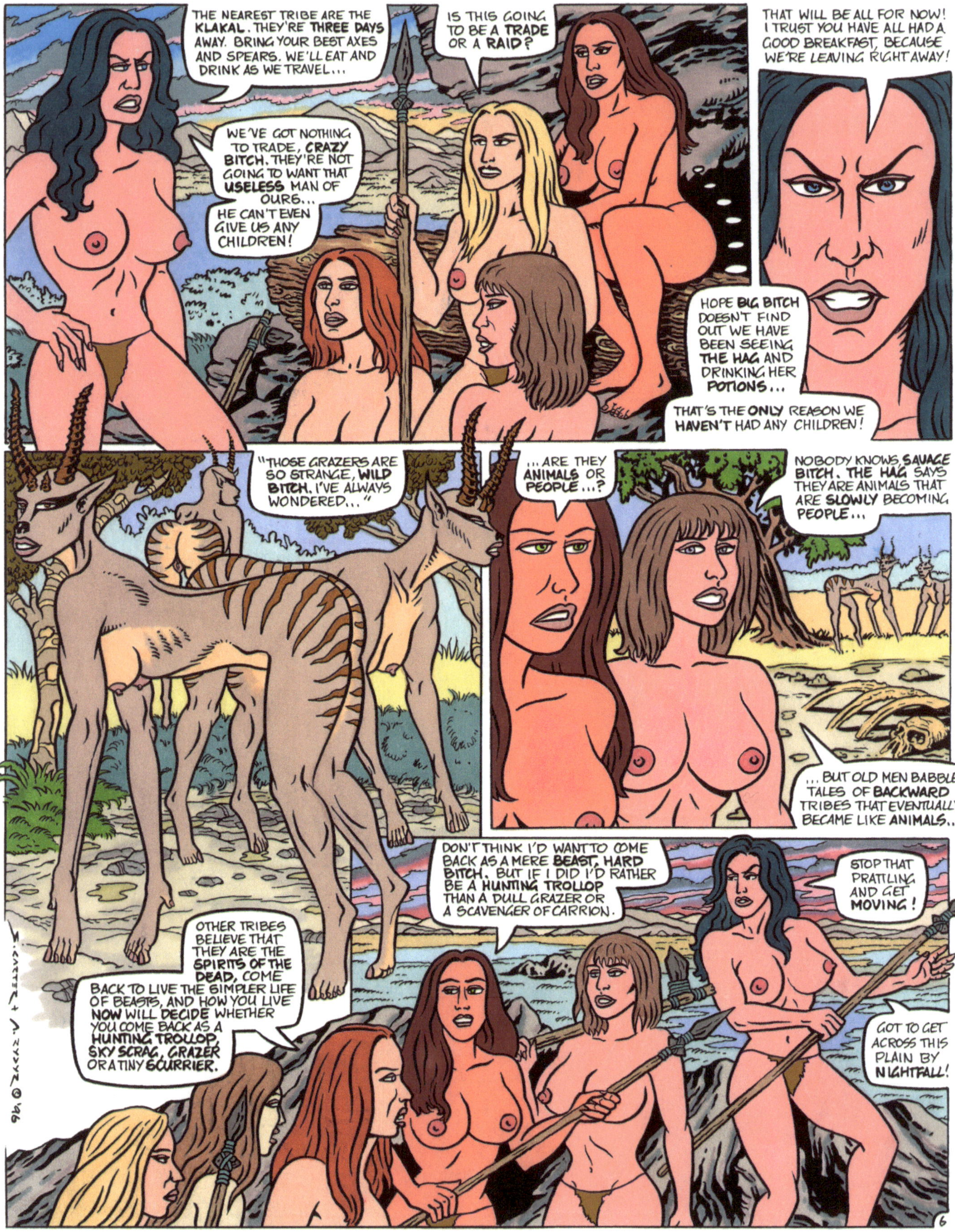

THE NEAREST TRIBE ARE THE KLAKAL. THEY'RE THREE DAYS AWAY. BRING YOUR BEST AXES AND SPEARS. WE'LL EAT AND DRINK AS WE TRAVEL...
WE'VE GOT NOTHING TO TRADE, CRAZY BITCH. THEY'RE NOT GOING TO WANT THAT USELESS MAN OF OURS... HE CAN'T EVEN GIVE US ANY CHILDREN!
IS THIS GOING TO BE A TRADE OR A RAID?
THAT WILL BE ALL FOR NOW! I TRUST YOU HAVE ALL HAD A GOOD BREAKFAST, BECAUSE WE'RE LEAVING RIGHT AWAY!
HOPE BIG BITCH DOESN'T FIND OUT WE HAVE BEEN SEEING THE HAG AND DRINKING HER POTIONS...
THAT'S THE ONLY REASON WE HAVEN'T HAD ANY CHILDREN!
"THOSE GRAZERS ARE SO STRANGE, WILD BITCH. I'VE ALWAYS WONDERED..."
"...ARE THEY ANIMALS OR PEOPLE...?"
NOBODY KNOWS, SAVAGE BITCH. THE HAG SAYS THEY ARE ANIMALS THAT ARE SLOWLY BECOMING PEOPLE...
...BUT OLD MEN BABBLE TALES OF BACKWARD TRIBES THAT EVENTUALLY BECAME LIKE ANIMALS...
OTHER TRIBES BELIEVE THAT THEY ARE THE SPIRITS OF THE DEAD, COME BACK TO LIVE THE SIMPLER LIFE OF BEASTS, AND HOW YOU LIVE NOW WILL DECIDE WHETHER YOU COME BACK AS A HUNTING TROLLOP, SKY SCRAG, GRAZER OR A TINY SCURRIER.
DON'T THINK I'D WANT TO COME BACK AS A MERE BEAST, HARD BITCH. BUT IF I DID I'D RATHER BE A HUNTING TROLLOP THAN A DULL GRAZER OR A SCAVENGER OF CARRION.
STOP THAT PRATTLING AND GET MOVING!
GOT TO GET ACROSS THIS PLAIN BY NIGHTFALL!

THERE ARE AT LEAST THREE DIFFERENT KINDS OF GRAZERS HERE... EVEN A COLD BLOOD!
"SOMETHING HAS STARTLED THEM ALL!"
JUST KEEP WATCHING THEM. IF THERE ARE ANY PREDATORS ABOUT, THEY'LL BE THE FIRST TO KNOW...
SPRINTING TROLLOPS!
WE'RE SAFE NOW. THEY'VE MADE THEIR KILL AND THEY'VE GOT THEIR FOOD.
QUICKLY! UP INTO THE COVER OF THOSE ROCKS ON THAT HILL.
...GOOD PLACE TO SPEND THE NIGHT... WE CAN SEE ALL 'ROUND AND IT'S EASY TO DEFEND.
S. CARTER A.ZYPVZ ©'95
7

IT IS GOING TO BE A LONG NIGHT AND ONE OF THESE TWILIGHT FLIERS' WILL MAKE A PERFECT FEAST!
BEING THAT YOU'RE THE YOUNGEST HUNTRESS HERE...
AND THAT THERE IS NO MAN WITH US...
YOU CAN GO AND GET THE CARCASS, SAVAGE BITCH,
YES!
BIG BITCH'S AIM IS TRUE!
AND BE SURE TO BRING BACK MY SPEAR!
OH NO!
A SPRINTING TROLLOP WANTS IT...
A FLEET FOOTED DEVIL TROLLOP?
MUST HAVE BEEN LURKING AMID THOSE ROCKS!
LOOKS LIKE THEY'RE GOING TO FIGHT FOR IT...
...BETTER BE QUICK!
NO DOUBT I'LL HAVE TO BUTCHER AND COOK IT AS WELL.
S. CARTER + AZZYZ ©'95

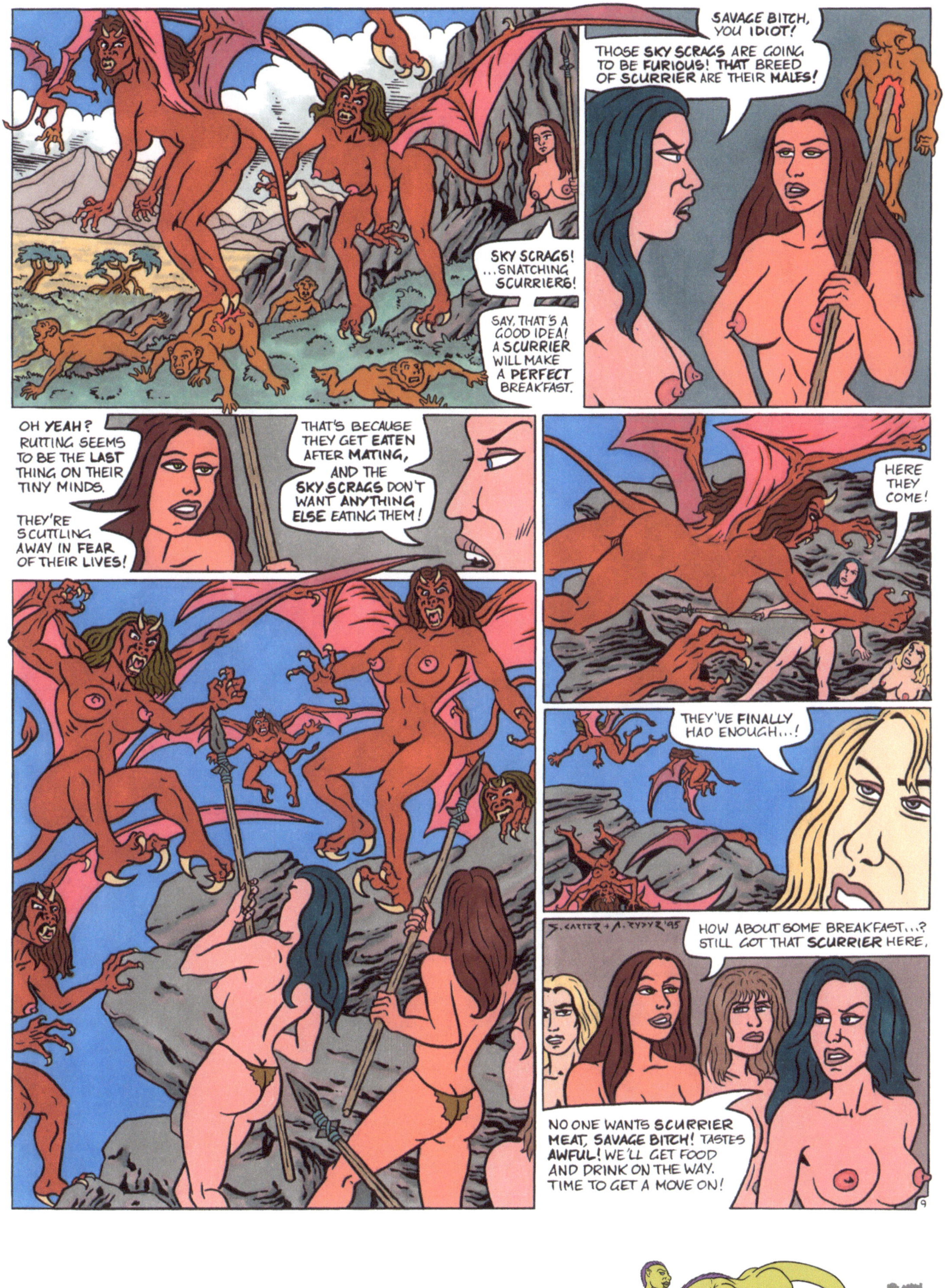

SAVAGE BITCH, YOU IDIOT!
THOSE SKY SCRAGS ARE GOING TO BE FURIOUS! THAT BREED OF SCURRIER ARE THEIR MALES!
SKY SCRAGS! ...SNATCHING SCURRIERS!
SAY, THAT'S A GOOD IDEA! A SCURRIER WILL MAKE A PERFECT BREAKFAST.
OH YEAH? RUTTING SEEMS TO BE THE LAST THING ON THEIR TINY MINDS.
THEY'RE SCUTTLING AWAY IN FEAR OF THEIR LIVES!
THAT'S BECAUSE THEY GET EATEN AFTER MATING, AND THE SKY SCRAGS DON'T WANT ANYTHING ELSE EATING THEM!
HERE THEY COME!
THEY'VE FINALLY HAD ENOUGH...!
S. CARTER + A. RYDER '95
HOW ABOUT SOME BREAKFAST...? STILL GOT THAT SCURRIER HERE,
NO ONE WANTS SCURRIER MEAT, SAVAGE BITCH! TASTES AWFUL! WE'LL GET FOOD AND DRINK ON THE WAY. TIME TO GET A MOVE ON!
9

THEY'RE MASSIVE!
HOW ARE WE GOING TO GET PAST THEM?
BY WALKING RIGHT PAST THEM. THEY WON'T CARE ABOUT US...
THEY'RE ONLY BROWSERS. JUST BE WARY OF THE OLD MALES. THEY'RE KNOWN TO CHARGE AT ANYTHING THAT GETS TOO CLOSE.
HOW MUCH FURTHER TO THE KLAKAL VILLAGE, NOW?
...SHOULD BE THERE BY THE FOLLOWING DUSK...
CROARHG!
BIG BITCH! WHY IS THAT ONE BELLOWING LIKE THAT...?!
S. CARTER T. MYRNE ©'96.
FIND COVER — NOW! IT'S A STAMPEDE!
SAVAGE BITCH, GET BACK!
10

16

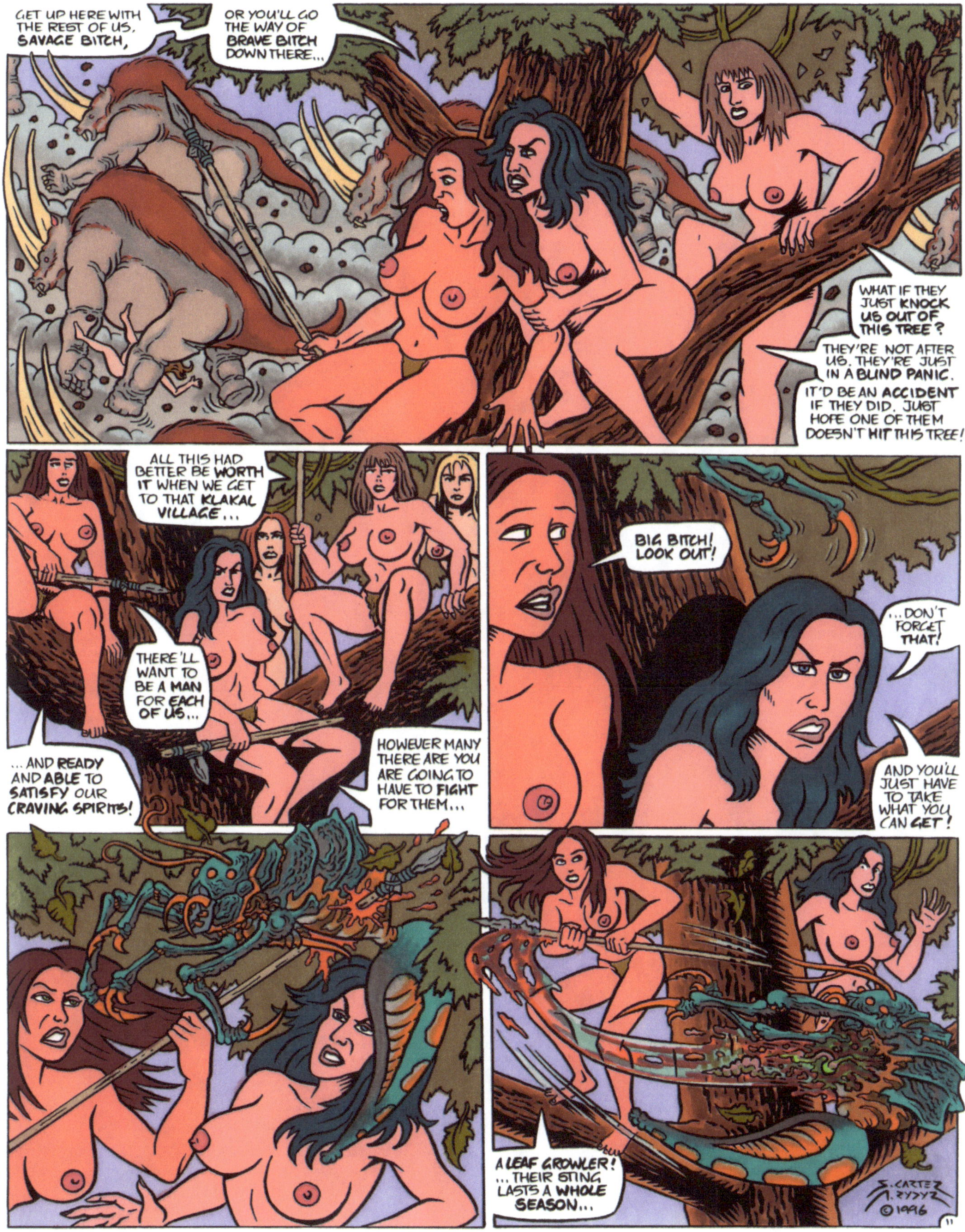

GET UP HERE WITH THE REST OF US, SAVAGE BITCH,
OR YOU'LL GO THE WAY OF BRAVE BITCH DOWN THERE...
WHAT IF THEY JUST KNOCK US OUT OF THIS TREE?
THEY'RE NOT AFTER US. THEY'RE JUST IN A BLIND PANIC. IT'D BE AN ACCIDENT IF THEY DID. JUST HOPE ONE OF THEM DOESN'T HIT THIS TREE!
ALL THIS HAD BETTER BE WORTH IT WHEN WE GET TO THAT KLAKAL VILLAGE...
THERE'LL WANT TO BE A MAN FOR EACH OF US...
...AND READY AND ABLE TO SATISFY OUR CRAVING SPIRITS!
HOWEVER MANY THERE ARE YOU ARE GOING TO HAVE TO FIGHT FOR THEM...
BIG BITCH! LOOK OUT!
...DON'T FORGET THAT!
AND YOU'LL JUST HAVE TO TAKE WHAT YOU CAN GET!
A LEAF GROWLER! ...THEIR STING LASTS A WHOLE SEASON...
S. CARTER A. ZYDYZ ©1996

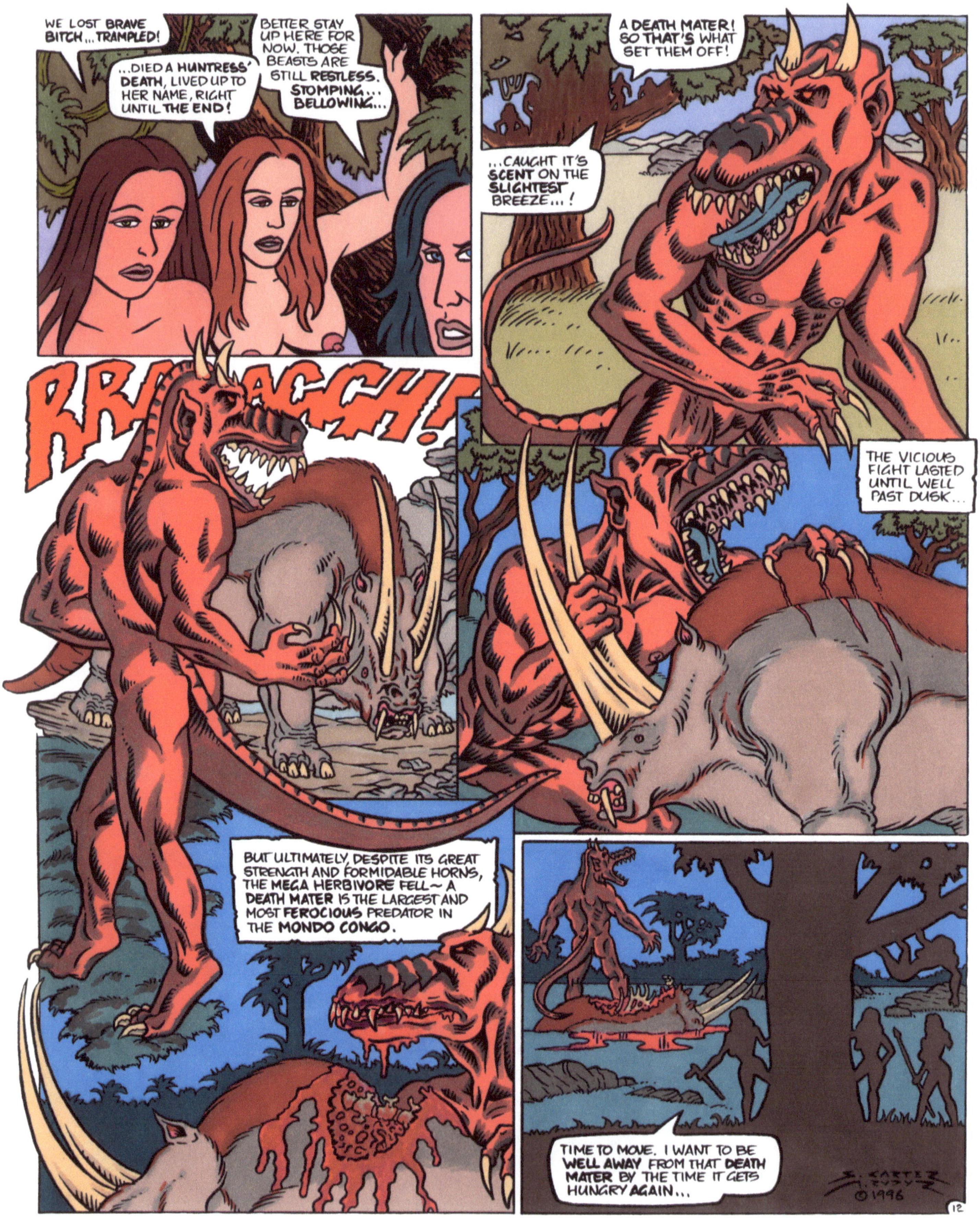

WE LOST BRAVE BITCH...TRAMPLED!
...DIED A HUNTRESS' DEATH, LIVED UP TO HER NAME, RIGHT UNTIL THE END!
BETTER STAY UP HERE FOR NOW. THOSE BEASTS ARE STILL RESTLESS. STOMPING... BELLOWING....
A DEATH MATER! SO THAT'S WHAT SET THEM OFF!
...CAUGHT IT'S SCENT ON THE SLIGHTEST BREEZE...!
RRRAAGGH!
THE VICIOUS FIGHT LASTED UNTIL WELL PAST DUSK...
BUT ULTIMATELY, DESPITE ITS GREAT STRENGTH AND FORMIDABLE HORNS, THE MEGA HERBIVORE FELL~ A DEATH MATER IS THE LARGEST AND MOST FEROCIOUS PREDATOR IN THE MONDO CONGO.
TIME TO MOVE. I WANT TO BE WELL AWAY FROM THAT DEATH MATER BY THE TIME IT GETS HUNGRY AGAIN...
S. CARTER
© 1996
12

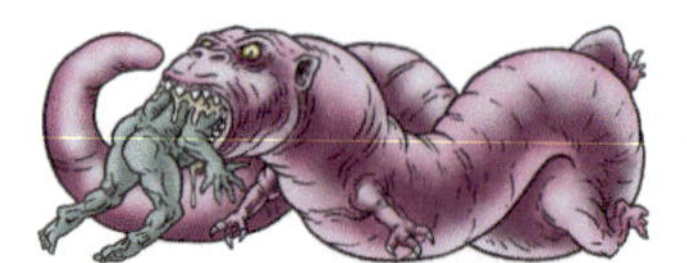

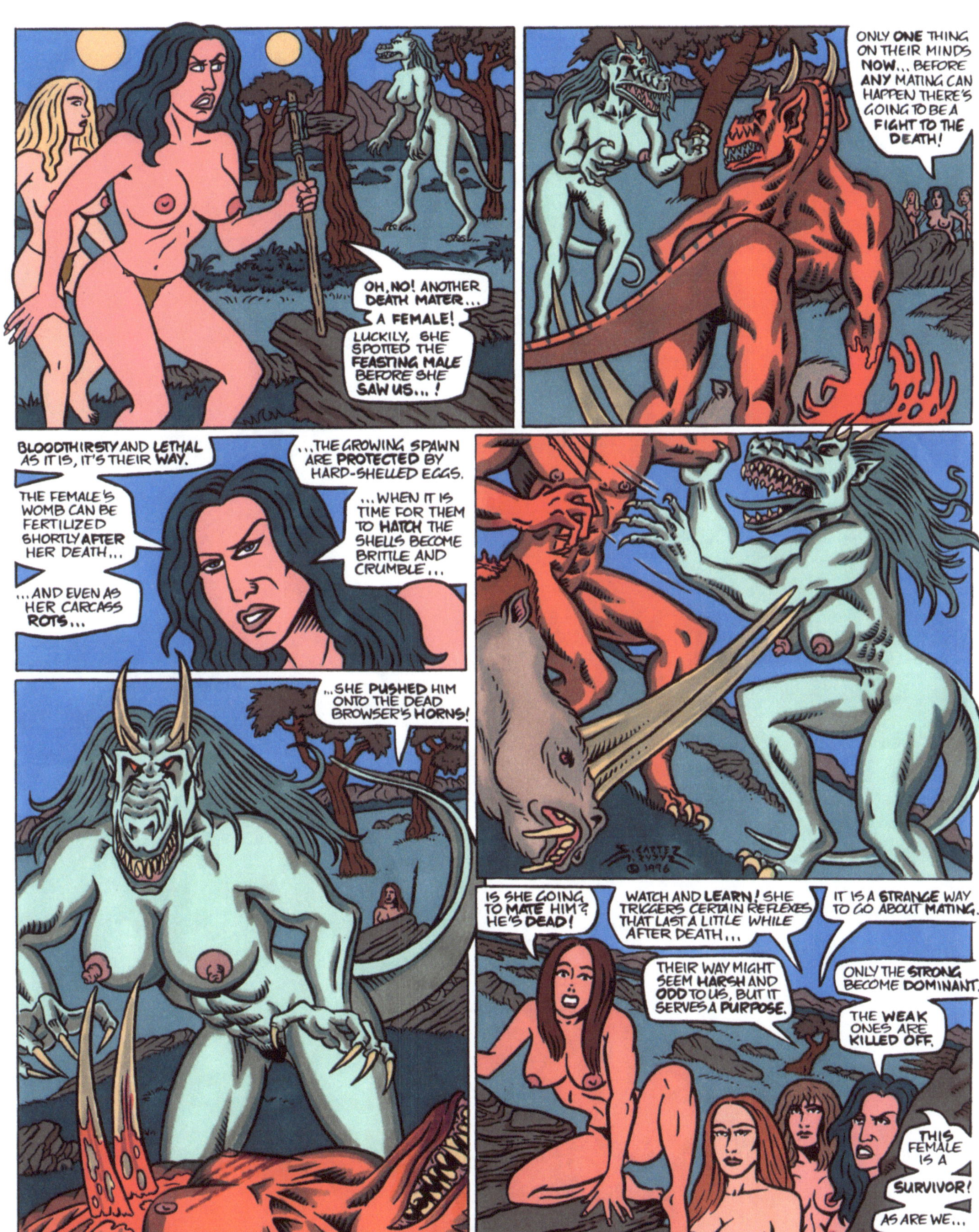

OH, NO! ANOTHER DEATH MATER... A FEMALE! LUCKILY, SHE SPOTTED THE FEASTING MALE BEFORE SHE SAW US...!
ONLY ONE THING ON THEIR MINDS NOW... BEFORE ANY MATING CAN HAPPEN THERE'S GOING TO BE A FIGHT TO THE DEATH!
BLOODTHIRSTY AND LETHAL AS IT IS, IT'S THEIR WAY.
THE FEMALE'S WOMB CAN BE FERTILIZED SHORTLY AFTER HER DEATH...
...AND EVEN AS HER CARCASS ROTS...
...THE GROWING SPAWN ARE PROTECTED BY HARD-SHELLED EGGS.
...WHEN IT IS TIME FOR THEM TO HATCH THE SHELLS BECOME BRITTLE AND CRUMBLE...
...SHE PUSHED HIM ONTO THE DEAD BROWSER'S HORNS!
IS SHE GOING TO MATE HIM? HE'S DEAD!
WATCH AND LEARN! SHE TRIGGERS CERTAIN REFLEXES THAT LAST A LITTLE WHILE AFTER DEATH...
IT IS A STRANGE WAY TO GO ABOUT MATING.
THEIR WAY MIGHT SEEM HARSH AND ODD TO US, BUT IT SERVES A PURPOSE.
ONLY THE STRONG BECOME DOMINANT.
THE WEAK ONES ARE KILLED OFF.
THIS FEMALE IS A SURVIVOR!
AS ARE WE...

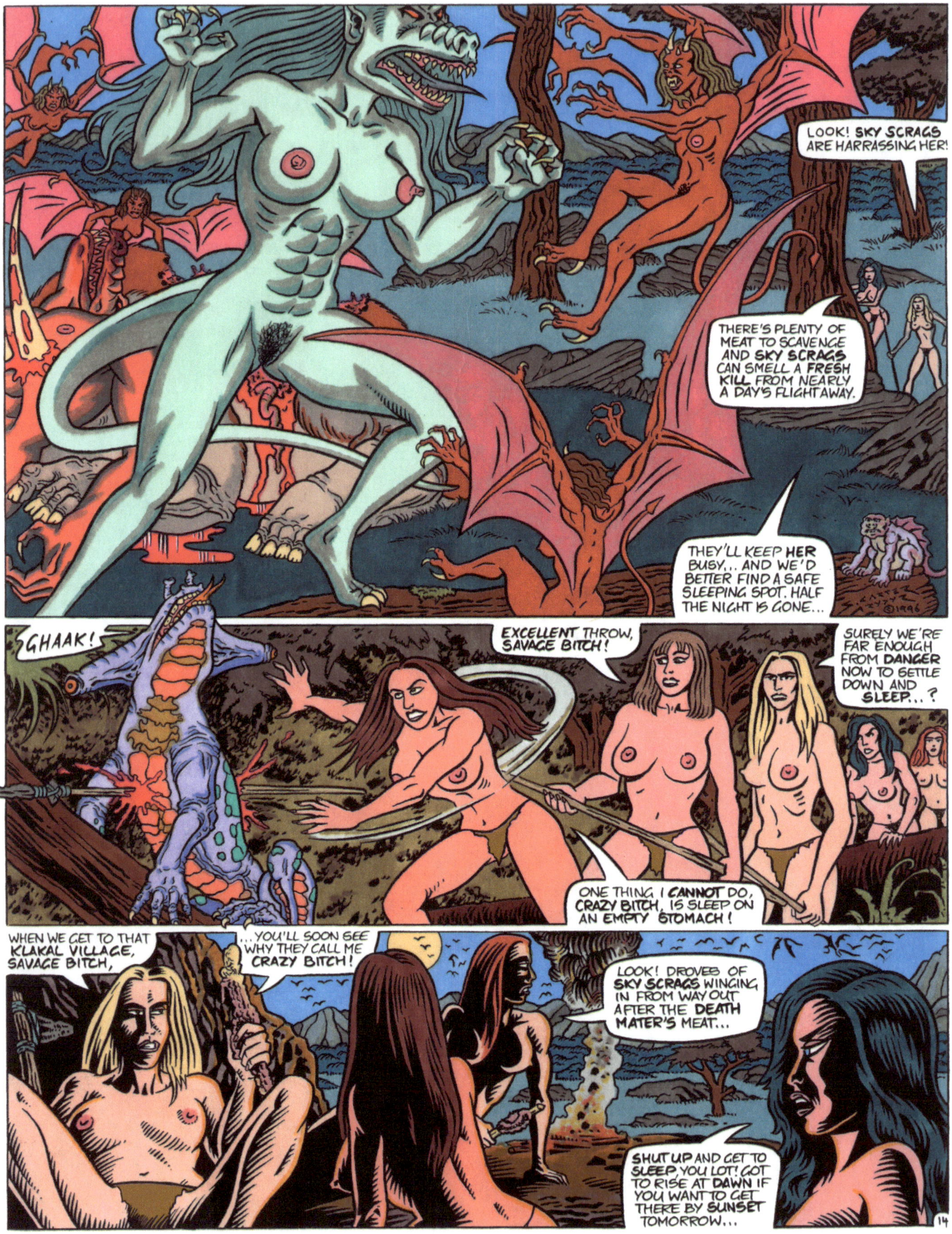

LOOK! SKY SCRAGS ARE HARRASSING HER!

THERE'S PLENTY OF MEAT TO SCAVENGE AND SKY SCRAGS CAN SMELL A FRESH KILL FROM NEARLY A DAY'S FLIGHT AWAY.

THEY'LL KEEP HER BUSY... AND WE'D BETTER FIND A SAFE SLEEPING SPOT. HALF THE NIGHT IS GONE...

GHAAK!

EXCELLENT THROW, SAVAGE BITCH!

SURELY WE'RE FAR ENOUGH FROM DANGER NOW TO SETTLE DOWN AND SLEEP...?

ONE THING I CANNOT DO, CRAZY BITCH, IS SLEEP ON AN EMPTY STOMACH!

WHEN WE GET TO THAT KLAKAL VILLAGE, SAVAGE BITCH,

...YOU'LL SOON SEE WHY THEY CALL ME CRAZY BITCH!

LOOK! DROVES OF SKY SCRAGS WINGING IN FROM WAY OUT AFTER THE DEATH MATER'S MEAT...

SHUT UP AND GET TO SLEEP, YOU LOT! GOT TO RISE AT DAWN IF YOU WANT TO GET THERE BY SUNSET TOMORROW...

14

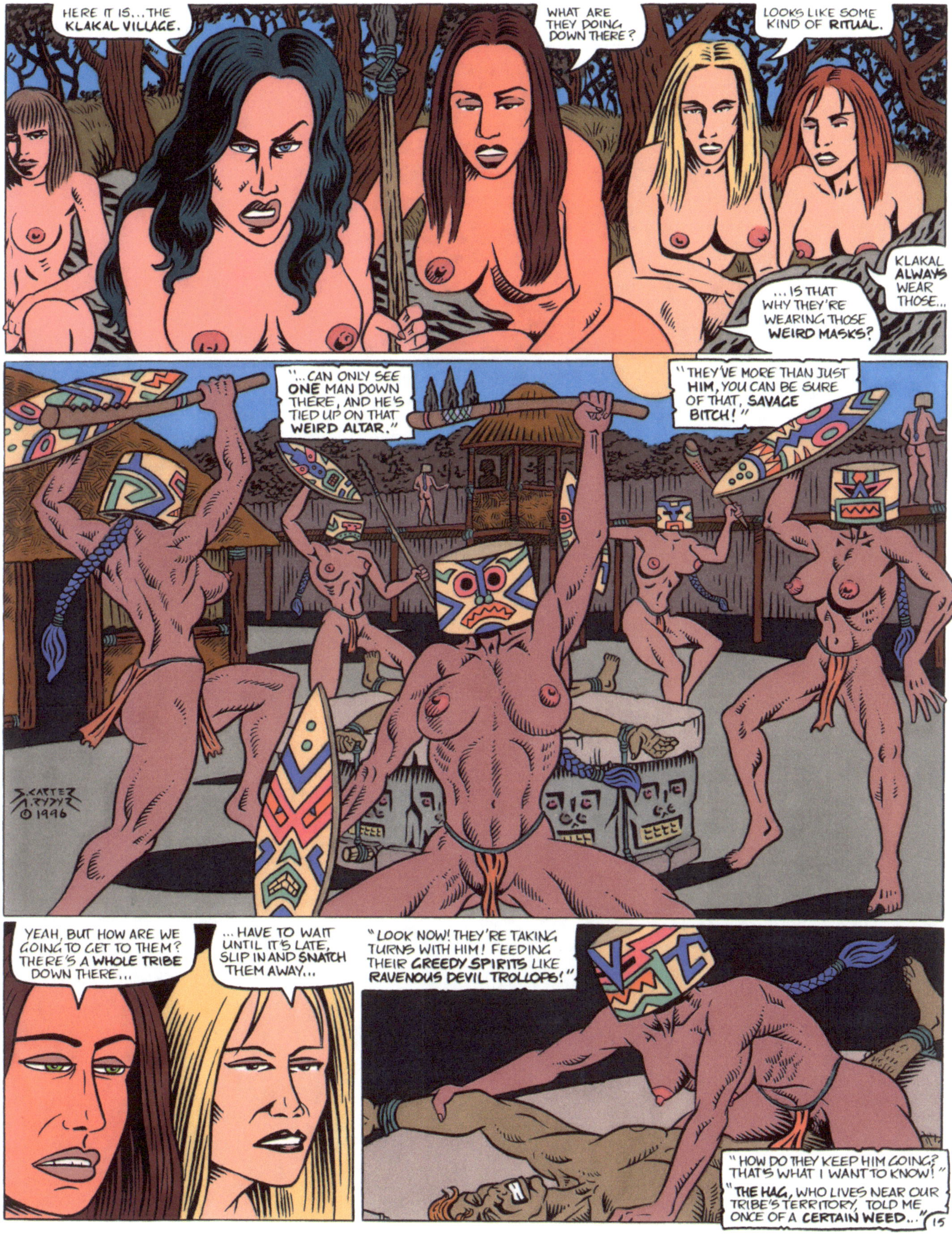

HERE IT IS...THE KLAKAL VILLAGE.
WHAT ARE THEY DOING DOWN THERE?
LOOKS LIKE SOME KIND OF RITUAL.
...IS THAT WHY THEY'RE WEARING THOSE WEIRD MASKS?
KLAKAL ALWAYS WEAR THOSE...

"...CAN ONLY SEE ONE MAN DOWN THERE, AND HE'S TIED UP ON THAT WEIRD ALTAR."
"THEY'VE MORE THAN JUST HIM, YOU CAN BE SURE OF THAT, SAVAGE BITCH!"

YEAH, BUT HOW ARE WE GOING TO GET TO THEM? THERE'S A WHOLE TRIBE DOWN THERE...
...HAVE TO WAIT UNTIL IT'S LATE, SLIP IN AND SNATCH THEM AWAY...
"LOOK NOW! THEY'RE TAKING TURNS WITH HIM! FEEDING THEIR GREEDY SPIRITS LIKE RAVENOUS DEVIL TROLLOPS!"
"HOW DO THEY KEEP HIM GOING? THAT'S WHAT I WANT TO KNOW!"
"THE HAG, WHO LIVES NEAR OUR TRIBE'S TERRITORY, TOLD ME ONCE OF A CERTAIN WEED..."
15

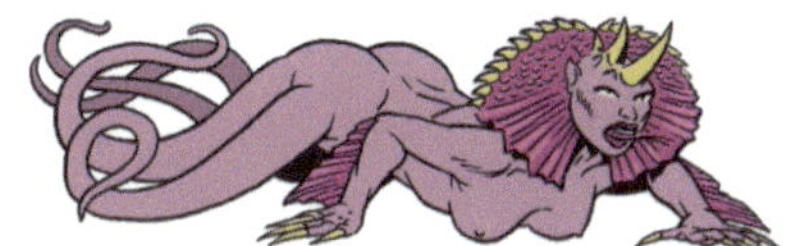

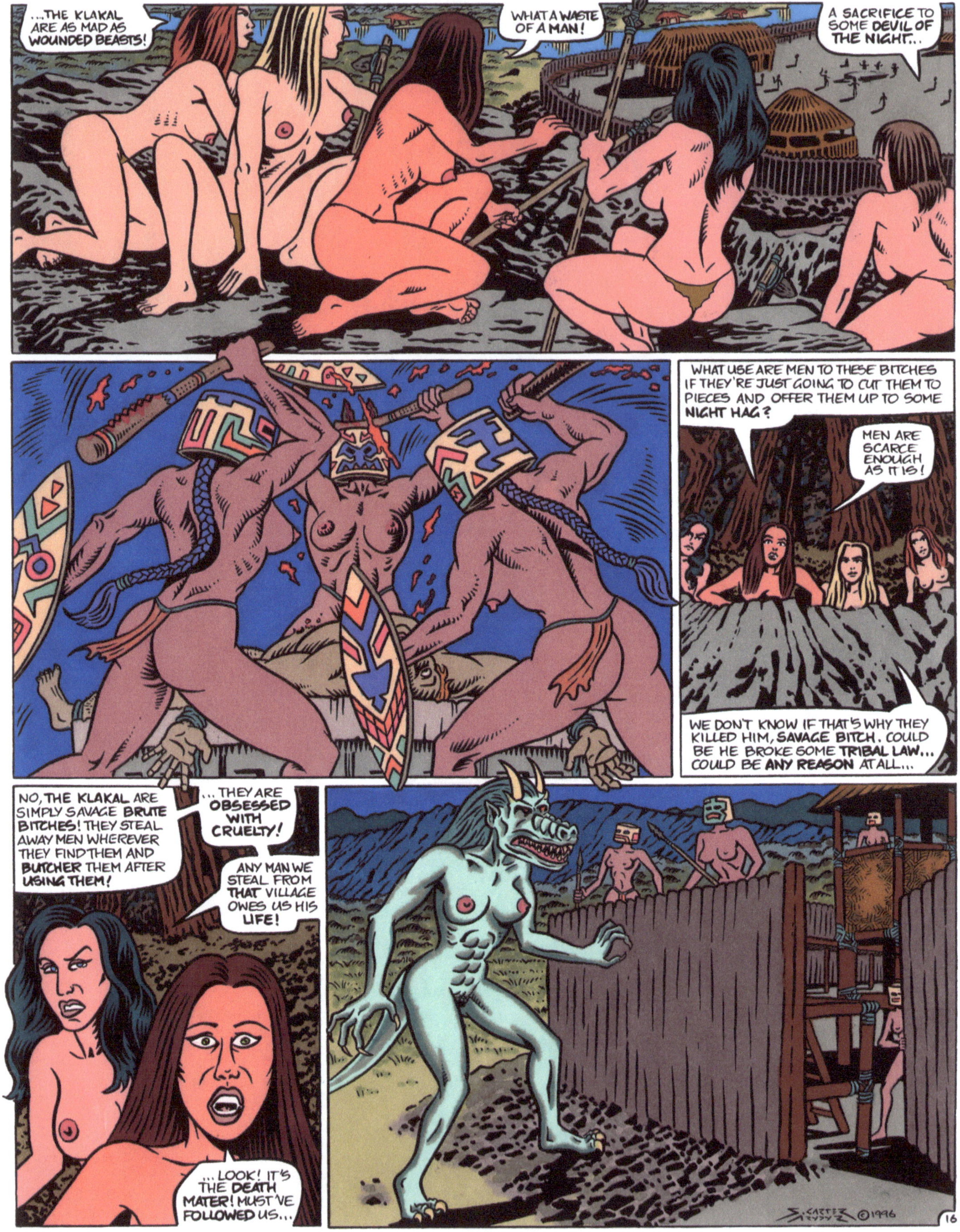

S. CARTER ©1996

16

TIME TO MOVE! LET'S GET DOWN THERE!
YOU WANT US TO GO DOWN AMONGST THAT LOT?
YES, SAVAGE BITCH! WE COULDN'T HAVE ASKED FOR A BETTER DISTRACTION. YOU WANT TO GET YOURSELF A MAN, DON'T YOU?

IT'S BROKEN INTO THE PENS FOR THE MEN...

...DEAD BODIES AND WRECKAGE!
GOOD! THE MORE DEAD KLAKAL, THE LESS WE HAVE TO FIGHT... NOW LET'S FIND US SOME MEN!

NOW WE KNOW WHO BROUGHT THE DEVIL BITCH DOWN ON OUR VILLAGE!
KILL THE INTRUDER BITCHES!

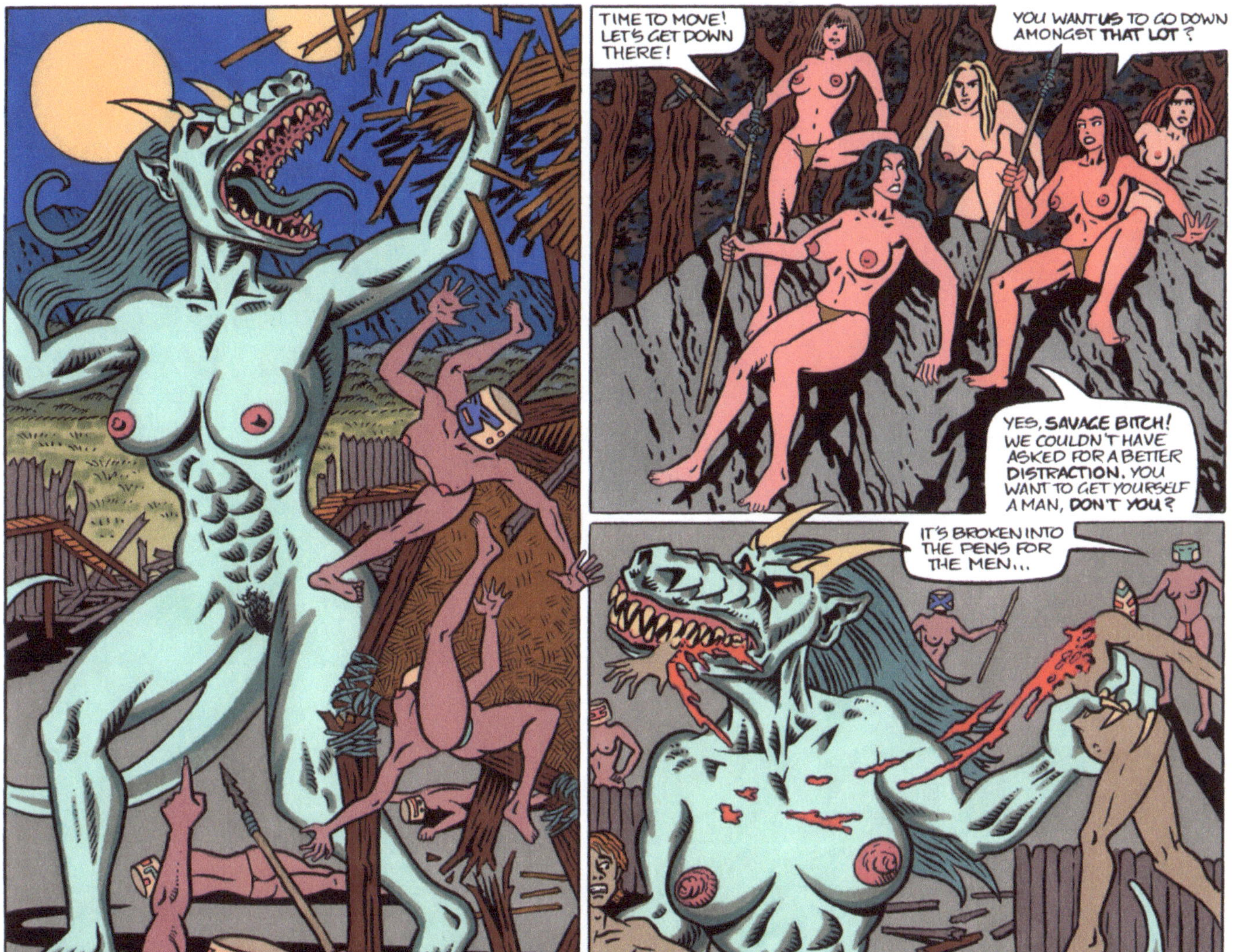

17

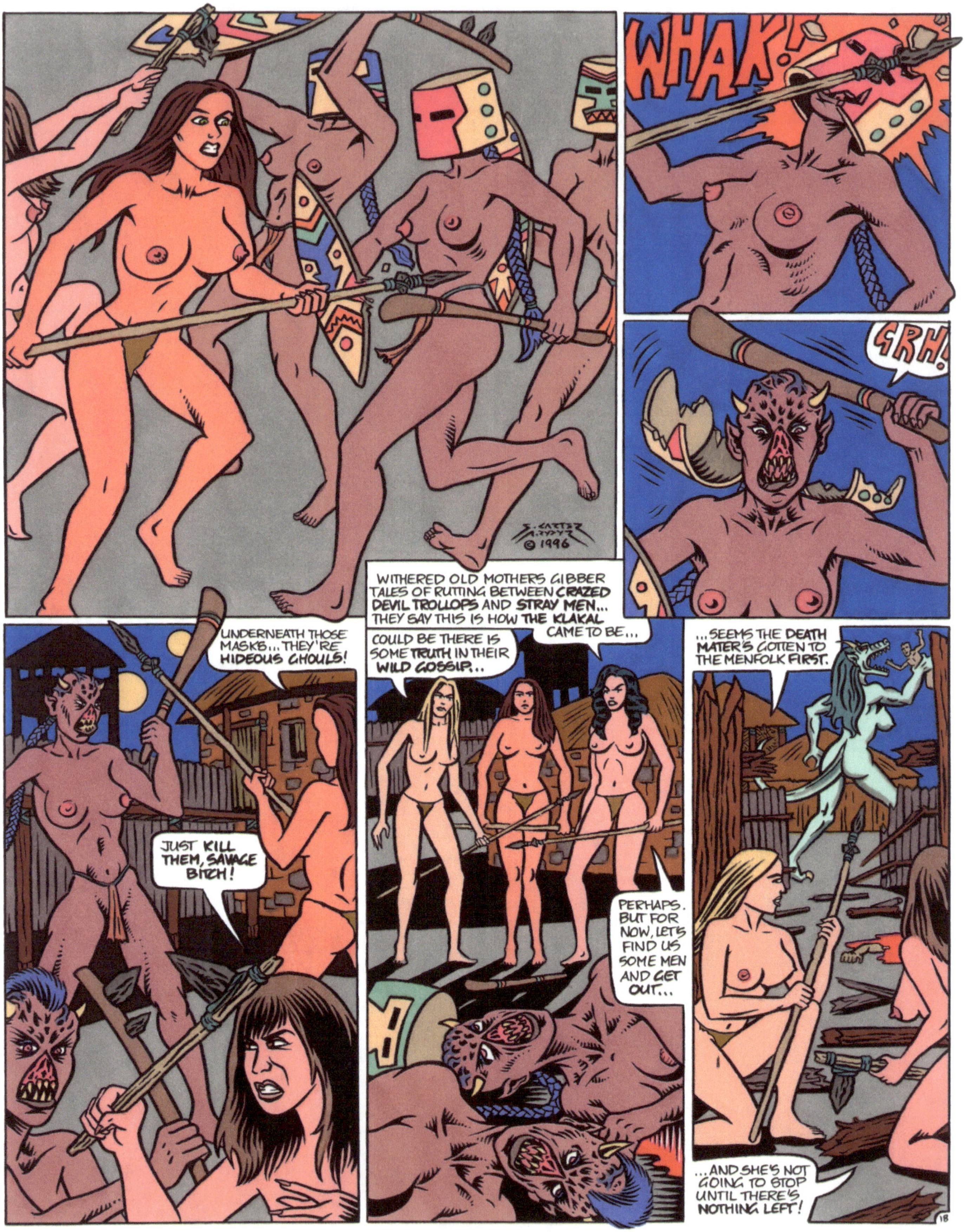

WHAK!
©1996
GRH!

WITHERED OLD MOTHERS GIBBER TALES OF RUTTING BETWEEN CRAZED DEVIL TROLLOPS AND STRAY MEN... THEY SAY THIS IS HOW THE KLAKAL CAME TO BE...
COULD BE THERE IS SOME TRUTH IN THEIR WILD GOSSIP...

UNDERNEATH THOSE MASKS... THEY'RE HIDEOUS GHOULS!
JUST KILL THEM, SAVAGE BIZH!

PERHAPS. BUT FOR NOW, LET'S FIND US SOME MEN AND GET OUT...

...SEEMS THE DEATH MATER'S GOTTEN TO THE MENFOLK FIRST.
...AND SHE'S NOT GOING TO STOP UNTIL THERE'S NOTHING LEFT!

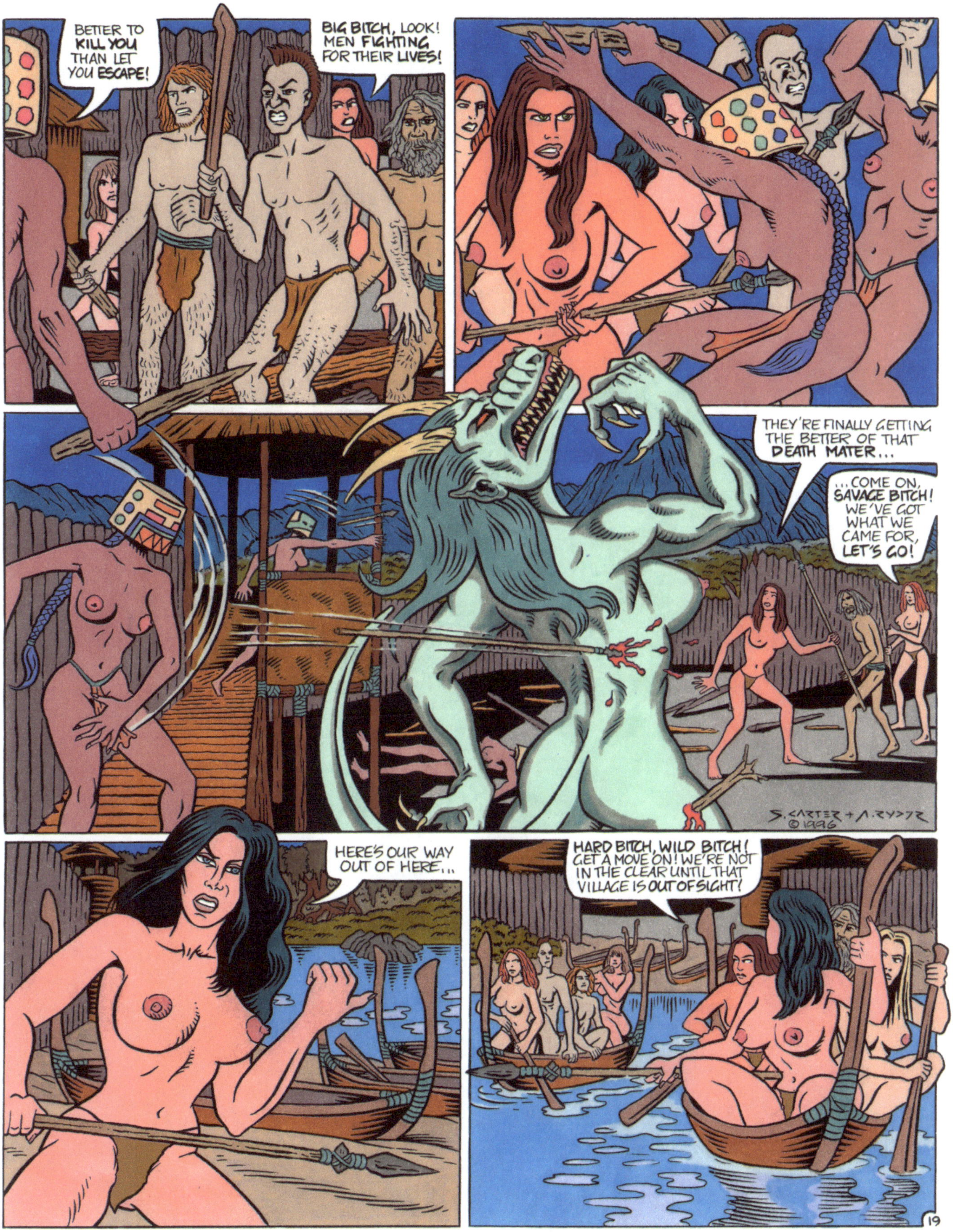

BETTER TO KILL YOU THAN LET YOU ESCAPE!
BIG BITCH, LOOK! MEN FIGHTING FOR THEIR LIVES!
THEY'RE FINALLY GETTING THE BETTER OF THAT DEATH MATER...
...COME ON, SAVAGE BITCH! WE'VE GOT WHAT WE CAME FOR, LET'S GO!
HERE'S OUR WAY OUT OF HERE...
HARD BITCH, WILD BITCH! GET A MOVE ON! WE'RE NOT IN THE CLEAR UNTIL THAT VILLAGE IS OUT OF SIGHT!
S. CARTER + A. RYDYR
© 1996

I'VE NEVER SEEN SO MANY SCURRIERS!
THERE'S MORE BREEDS OF SCURRIER ON THIS WORLD THAN ANYTHING ELSE, SAVAGE BITCH.

...URGH! SLITHERERS! THEY'RE IRKSOME!
YOU THINK UP THE MOST HORRIBLE OF FATES, HARD BITCH...!
IMAGINE COMING BACK AS ONE OF THOSE IN YOUR NEXT LIFE!
S. CARTER A. RYDYR

LOOK AT THAT! SWALLOWING IT WHOLE!
FORGET THAT SLITHERER, WILD BITCH. LOOK WHAT'S COMING UP BEHIND US!

THERE THEY ARE!
THE ONES WHO BROUGHT THE DEVIL BITCH DOWN ON OUR VILLAGE AND STOLE THE MEN!
KILL THEM ALL!

KLAKAL BEHIND US, MUD WALLOWERS IN FRONT,...
NICE AND SLOW DOES IT, CRAZY BITCH. WE'LL GET PAST...

THOSE KLAKAL ARE CLOSING FAST,...
KEEP IT STEADY. WE'RE ALMOST THROUGH THEM.
20

26

THAT MUD WALLOWER HAS GONE WILD!
AAIEEH!
THAT'S THE BIGGEST TOADLING I'VE EVER SEEN!
IT'S GOBBLING THEM ALL UP, ONE BY ONE!
S. CARTER + A. RYDYR '96
... WHAT IS BUKU BUKU?
A STORY OLD HAGS USE TO SCARE THE YOUNG. THIS PLACE IS NO MORE DANGEROUS THAN ANYWHERE ELSE WE HAVE BEEN.
IT'S A DANGEROUS WORLD AND ONLY THE BEST SURVIVE.
WE SHOULD GO ANOTHER WAY. THIS IS A BAD REGION. GIANT TOADLINGS, SWAMPIES, SLITHERERS BIG ENOUGH TO EAT A FULLY GROWN MAN,
AND WORST OF ALL, THE BUKU BUKU, MORE DEADLY THAN THE KLAKAL!
RIGHT NOW, WE FIND SOMEWHERE TO REST AND EAT. IT'S NEARLY MORNING.
21

SAVAGE BITCH
- IN THE LAND OF THE BUKU BUKU
PART TWO
SCAR 2008
STORY & ART © 1995-2008 STEVE CARTER & ANTOINETTE RYDYR (S.C.A.R)

DON'T WANT TO DO IT WITH YOU. DO IT WITH HER...
BETTER GET IT STRAIGHT! YOU HAVE NO SAY. YOU JUST DO WHAT YOU'RE TOLD TO DO, OR ELSE!
MAKE HIM DO IT WITH ALL OF US. TEACH HIM TO BE TOO FUSSY!
THEY'LL ALL BE DOING THAT, ANYWAY, CRAZY BITCH!
WHAT DIFFERENCE DOES IT MAKE WHO HE DOES IT WITH? YOU WANT A MAN, WELL, HERE I AM!
YOU'RE NOT GOOD ENOUGH TO TELL ME WHAT TO DO!
WOOSH!
THAK!
BETTER OFF LEAVING THAT ONE BACK WITH THE KLAKAL, BIG BITCH!
SHUT UP AND GO ABUSE ONE OF THE OTHER MEN, SAVAGE BITCH! THAT'S WHAT WE GOT THEM FOR!
YOU WIN, I'M YOURS.
FOR NOW...
MANFLESH! I SMELL MANFLESH!
THE SWAMP MOTHER IS HUNGRY FOR THE SEED OF A MAN
...AND WE FOR HIS FLESH!
I HAVE FOUND THE MANFLESH!
OOOH, YES! WHAT A LONG, PERFECTLY LAZY DAY IT IS...
A GIRL'S SPIRIT IS FINALLY AS FULL AS HER STOMACH!
RUTTING YOU GIRLS IS SUCH PLEASURE AFTER THE KLAKAL!
S. CARTER + ARYYYR © '96
22

SCURRIERS! FLEEING IN A PANIC!
SOMETHING HAS STIRRED THEM UP...
SOMETHING SMELLS, AND IT'S NOT THIS FISH...
SWAMPIES!
YOU TAKE FROM SWAMP MOTHER, YOU GIVE SOMETHING BACK IN RETURN!
...GIVE US MANFLESH!
SWAMP MOTHER WANTS HIS SEED
SWACK!
THESE SWAMPIES ARE WEAKLINGS!
ONE GOOD WHOLLOP AND THEY GO DOWN!
THAT MAY BE SO, BIG BITCH, BUT THERE ARE TOO MANY OF THEM!
DON'T LET THEM SCRATCH YOU... THE STING DRIVES YOU INSANE AND SENDS YOU INTO A RUTTING FEVER!
AAIIEE! THE PAIN! CAN'T MOVE!
S. CARTER
© 1996
23

THEY ARE LIKE A SWARM!
CAN'T GET TO THE BOATS!
NOTHING YOU CAN DO FOR HIM...

GOT TO GET AWAY FROM THEM, NOW!
...BEFORE WE ALL END UP LIKE HIM!

I'VE NEVER SEEN SUCH FEVERISH RUTTING!
HE IS STRUCK BY A MADNESS THAT HAS HIM CRAVING ONLY FOR THOSE HORRIBLE SWAMPIES!
S. CARTER + A. RYDYR ©1996.

ONLY BY SEEDING US ALL CAN HE SEED THE WOMB OF THE SWAMP MOTHER!
HE IS NOT ENOUGH! THE SWAMP MOTHER NEEDS MORE!
GET AS FAR FROM THE RIVER AS WE CAN...
24

SEEDING WITH THIS ONE IS DONE!
NOW, WE FEED ON MANFLESH.
YAAHG!
AAAAAIIIEEEEGGGHH!!
THOSE DREADFUL SCREAMS, BIG BITCH!
WHAT ARE THEY DOING TO THAT POOR MAN?
...SAME THING THEY'LL DO TO US, SAVAGE BITCH, IF THEY CATCH US!
...THIS WAY LEADS OUT OF THE SWAMPS, I THINK...
...SO KEEP RUNNING!
THEY'LL GIVE UP ONCE WE LEAVE THEIR TERRITORY.
TIME TO JOIN OUR SISTERS IN THE CHASE AGAIN...
THERE IS STILL MANFLESH TO CATCH AND FLESH TO EAT...
S. CARTER
© 1996
THEY'RE RIGHT BEHIND US!
GRABBERS! SPAWNING IN THE MUD. IT'S WHEN THEY'RE AT THEIR MOST AGGRESSIVE.
THEY NEED BLOOD TO REPRODUCE...
25

LEAVE THEM! ...BEFORE ANY MORE OF US FALL INTO THE GRABBERS!
THEY WILL DIE ANYWAY. THE BUKU BUKU WILL SOON CLAIM THEM!
UGH! THEY'RE STABBING THEM WITH THEIR POINTY SHELLS! PULLING THEM APART AND BATHING IN THE SPILLING BLOOD!
HURRY UP, WILD BITCH, WE'RE GOING!
THAT IS THE ONLY WAY GRABBERS CAN SPAWN, ...IN WARM BLOOD!
26

WATCH OUT! IF IT SCRATCHES YOU THE VENOM WILL MAKE YOU VERY SICK. THEY'VE BEEN KNOWN TO CRAWL ALL OVER THEIR VICTIMS IN A GREAT, WRITHING MASS...
DRAINING THEM OF BLOOD AS THEY SPAWN...
THESE SORT USED TO BE EVERYWHERE NEAR THE VILLAGE I LIVED IN WHEN I WAS A BOY...
IF YOU'RE QUICK, YOU CAN PICK THEM UP, HOLD THEM LIKE THIS. ME AND THE OTHER BOYS USED TO DO IT ALL THE TIME.
WHENEVER WE FOUND THEM WE HAD TO KILL THEM. WE TURNED IT INTO A GAME...
WE'D POINT THEM AT ONE ANOTHER AND SQUEEZE!
YOU IDIOT! DO THAT AGAIN, YOU'RE DEAD!
SKAK!
IF IT WASN'T FOR WHAT WE WENT THROUGH TO GET THEM, AND THAT MEN ARE SO RARE, I'D HAVE KILLED HIM FOR THAT. I'M LEAVING HIM IN YOUR CARE, SAVAGE BITCH, AND YOU BETTER SEE THAT HE STAYS IN LINE!
YOU'RE SUCH A BIG BITCH, BIG BITCH!

HOW ARE WE GOING TO FIND A SAFE PLACE TO SLEEP WITH SO MANY GRABBERS AROUND?
WHAT GETS ME IS HOW DO YOU TELL THE MALES FROM THE FEMALES?
YOU'VE GOT ME THERE, CRAZY BITCH.
WHATEVER WE DO, AT LEAST TWO OF US ARE GOING TO HAVE TO BE ON WATCH ALL NIGHT LONG. WE'LL DO IT IN SHIFTS, WITH EACH OF US TAKING TURNS.
THEY AREN'T MALE OR FEMALE, OR MAYBE THEY'RE BOTH. ALL I KNOW IS THAT IF YOU GET TWO OF THEM TOGETHER AND BLOOD IS SPILLED THEY'LL RUT.
UP THERE, UNDER THAT ROCKY SHELF. THAT'S WHERE WE'LL SPEND THE NIGHT.
THERE'S STILL THE MATTER OF FOOD.
DON'T YOU WORRY ABOUT THAT, SAVAGE BITCH.
WE'LL FIND SOMETHING...
...TIME FOR YOU TWO TO ACT LIKE MEN. GET OVER HERE!
YOU AND CRAZY BITCH HAVE BEEN WITH THE MEN HALF THE NIGHT! WHEN DO THE REST OF US GET OUR SHARE?
AREN'T YOU MEANT TO BE ON WATCH DUTY WITH HARD BITCH?
BETTER GET TO IT, SAVAGE BITCH!
WHAT CAN THAT BE? ...CRASHING THROUGH THE BUSHES LIKE THAT...
IT'S HUGE, WHATEVER IT IS...

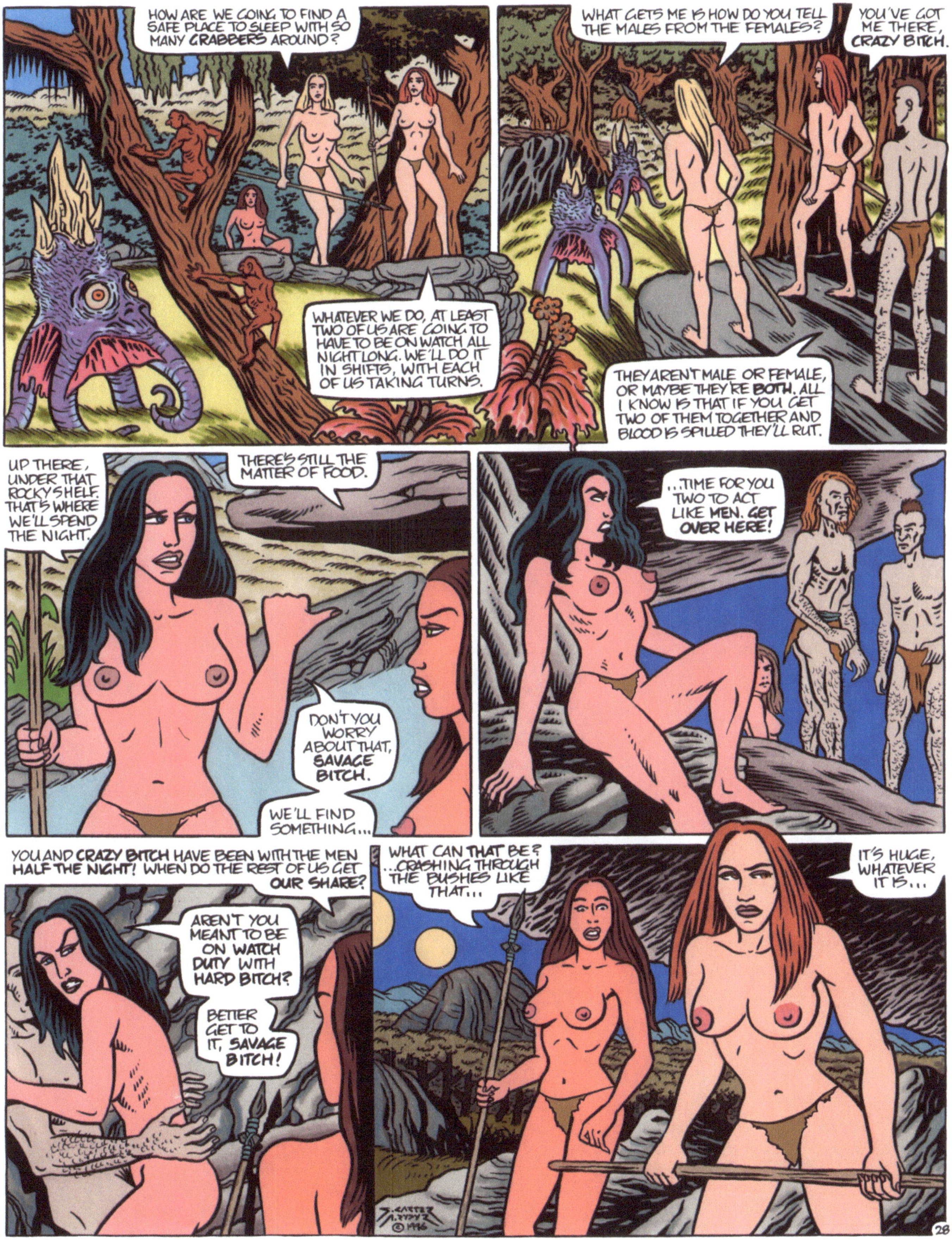

28

A GIANT GRABBER HAS SNATCHED UP HARD BITCH!
...GOT TO STOP IT BEFORE SHE'S TORN APART!
RRHG!

YOU ALRIGHT, HARD BITCH?
I THINK SO, WILD BITCH, NOTHING SEEMS BROKEN...
HOPE THERE'S EDIBLE MEAT ON THIS THING. SUN'S RISING AND I'M HUNGRY.
YOU'LL FIND THE FLESH FROM ITS LIMBS GOOD FOR THE COOKING FIRE.
...GOOD THROW! GOOD AS ANY WOMAN!
LET ME TELL YOU SOMETHING, SAVAGE BITCH! NO MAN IS EVER AS GOOD AS A WOMAN AT ANYTHING! I DON'T WANT TO HEAR YOU SAY ANYTHING THAT STUPID AGAIN! UNDERSTAND?
UM... YEAH!
YOU KNOW, SAVAGE BITCH, BIG BITCH IS RIGHT. YOU START TELLING THE MENFOLK THINGS LIKE THAT IT WILL ONLY ENCOURAGE THEM TO GET STUPID IDEAS ABOUT CHANGING THEIR LOT, AND WE DON'T WANT THAT!
...BESIDES, MEN ARE TOO FOOLISH TO DO ANYTHING ELSE BUT WHAT WE TELL THEM. AS IT IS, THERE'S NOTHING WORSE THAN A SMART MAN — LIKE THIS PAIR WE GOT WITH US NOW...
YOU BEEN HERE BEFORE, BIG BITCH? WE'RE LOST, AREN'T WE?
NOT AT ALL, SAVAGE BITCH. THIS MAY BE A STRANGE REGION BUT I NEVER LOSE MY SENSE OF DIRECTION OR KNOWLEDGE OF TIME AND DISTANCE. TRAITS ALL GOOD HUNTRESSES MUST LEARN WELL.
WE ARE ONLY ABOUT SIX DAYS' WALKING FROM HOME. FROM HERE, ALL WE HAVE TO DO IS GO STRAIGHT ACROSS THE FLOOD PLAINS. THEY'RE JUST BEYOND THAT RISE OUT THERE.
WE'VE A LONG TRIP AHEAD OF US. TIME TO MAKE A MOVE.
THIS WAY WILL TAKE US RIGHT INTO THE BUKU BUKU!
MAYBE SO, BUT IT'S THE QUICKEST WAY BACK FROM HERE.
UP THERE, LOOK! ARE THEY WINGED SCURRIERS OR SKY SCRAGS?
THEY'RE ONLY WINGED SCURRIERS AND ARE NOT DANGEROUS AT ALL
CARTER SNYDER © 1996

30

37

WHAT IS THIS PLACE?
THIS WAS BUILT BY THE BUKU BUKU IN TIMES LONG PAST. THEY WERE HERE WAY BEFORE MY PEOPLE CAME...
WHAT IS THE MEANING OF THESE IMAGES?
THE BUKU BUKU SUFFER A MADNESS OF BODY AND SOUL AND THEY CARVED IT INTO THE VERY STONES THEY USED TO BUILD THEIR DWELLINGS.
THIS PLACE FEELS VERY STRANGE.
WHATEVER MADNESS THAT POSSESSED THOSE WHO ONCE LIVED HERE IS LONG GONE NOW...
THERE ARE ONLY RUINS HERE NOW, SAVAGE BITCH. NOTHING TO BE AFRAID OF...
STRANGE AS THIS REGION IS, THOSE LONGNECKS OVER THERE ARE A FAMILIAR ENOUGH SIGHT.
THEY CERTAINLY ARE, HARD BITCH.
THOSE TWO COWS LOOK LIKE THEY'RE GOING TO ATTACK THAT COW!
THAT'S BECAUSE THEY HAVE NO DESIRE TO SHARE THEIR BULL WITH HER,
SHE'S NOT ONE OF THE HAREM.

S. CARTER
A. RYYYZ
© '96

RRRR!
GRRRH!
THAT BULL PREFERS THE NEW COW TO HIS OWN...
...AND THEY'RE NOT IMPRESSED. BE LIKE SEEING ONE OF OUR MEN RUN OFF WITH ANOTHER TRIBE.
...HIS OWN COWS ARE ATTACKING HIM!
THAT'S THEIR WAY OF TELLING HIM HE DOESN'T NEED ANY MORE COWS AND THAT HE SHOULD PAY ATTENTION ONLY TO THEM—NOT THAT OTHER ONE. THEY HATE REJECTION!
THEY ARE SO SAVAGE!
AND SO CAN WE BE WHEN IT COMES TO PULLING A STRAY MAN BACK IN LINE.
TRUE ENOUGH, HARD BITCH, BUT MOST FLESH-EATING HUNTING TROLLOPS ARE SELDOM AS VICIOUS...
WHEN IT COMES TO CLAIMING MATES OR DEFENDING TERRITORY, MANY GRAZERS CAN BE AS AGGRESSIVE AS ANY MEAT-EATER!
DID YOU KNOW, CRAZY BITCH, THAT LONGNECKS AND OTHER GRAZERS HAVE CLAIMED MORE LIVES THAN HUNTING BEASTS? YOU CAN'T BE TOO CAUTIOUS IN THE WILDERNESS.
BEST THAT WE GET UP HERE OUT OF THEIR WAY WITH THE OTHERS...

THOSE LONGNECKS ARE PUTTING ON QUITE A SHOW...
NOW THAT THEIR AGGRESSION'S UP IT'S TOO DANGEROUS TO GO ANYWHERE NEAR THEM.
SEEING THAT THERE'S LONG-NECKS EVERY-WHERE YOU LOOK, THAT MEANS WE'RE STUCK UP HERE FOR THE NIGHT.
S. CARTER J. RYDYR © 1996
OH, NO! LOOK OVER THERE!
A PACK OF HUNTING HOPPERS! ...THE SITUATION JUST GOT WORSE!
IT'S A TOTAL BLOOD BATH DOWN THERE!
33
40

S. CARTER
I. RYDYZ
©1996

RHAGH!

...WE'RE GOING TO HAVE TO FIGHT HARD TO GET OUT OF THIS ONE!

STAY CLOSE!

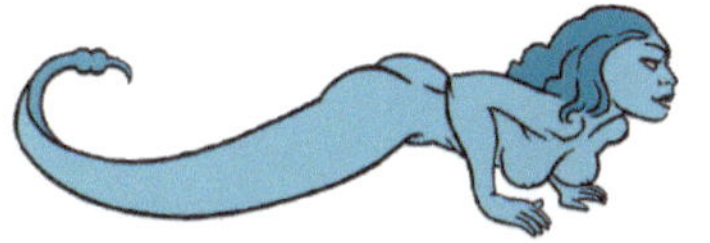

GET IN UNDER THE COVER OF THE TREES OUT OF SIGHT.
HURRY!
...RUINS EVERYWHERE!
GOOD! PROVIDE US WITH SHELTER FOR THE NIGHTS... FLOOD-PLAINS ARE STILL A COUPLE OF DAYS AWAY YET...
HEARD SOMETHING JUST OVER THERE...
DOWN IN THAT CAVE! ...BUKU BUKU!
...YOU SHALL SEED THE WOMB OF OKUGU MY LITTLE PIECE OF MAN MEAT!
...AND YOUR BITCHES CAN FILL HER STOMACH!
S. CARTER T. RYYYZ
© 1996

42

S. CARTER A. RYYYZ ©1996

36

43

...ALL I KNOW IS THAT THEY'RE A SPECIES OF DEVIL TROLLOPS THAT WENT TRIBAL. THAT'S THE STORY MY PEOPLE ALWAYS TELL...
TRIBAL DEVIL TROLLOPS? NEVER HEARD OF SUCH A WEIRD THING!
TRUE ENOUGH.
NOW TELL ME, WHERE IS THE BUKU BUKU VILLAGE?
I BELIEVE IT'S OVER THAT WAY, NEAR THAT BIG VOLCANO...
SOUNDS STRANGE, I KNOW. BUT YOU HAVE JUST SEEN ONE OF THEM — EVEN HEARD IT SPEAK...
GET THERE BY ZENITH TOMORROW — EASY!
HOW DO YOU EXPECT TO STEAL THAT MAN AWAY FROM A WHOLE VILLAGE OF THEM WHEN JUST ONE ALMOST KILLED ALL OF US, BIG BITCH?
WE WILL FIND A WAY, SAVAGE BITCH, BUT RIGHT NOW IT IS TIME TO RECOUPE OUR STRENGTH...
...WE ARE GOING TO NEED ALL WE HAVE FOR TOMORROW.
LOOK WHAT I HAVE CAUGHT! SNATCHED HIM RIGHT FROM HIS BITCHES!
YOU HAVE DONE WELL, YOUNG ULA. HE IS ONE OF THE LITTLE RACES, AND EVEN IF THEY DON'T GIVE US DAUGHTERS THEY MAKE GOOD RUTTING!
YES! THEY ARE MY FAVORITE!
YES! THE GROUND IS MOVING AT MY VERY FEET AND MY BODY AND LEGS QUIVER SO...
IT HAS PUT ME IN THE MOOD FOR RUTTING RIGHT NOW!
THE WAY THEY SHOUT AND WRIGGLE AND SQUEAL AND SQUIRM ALWAYS EXCITES ME!
...GREAT OKLUGU IS EXCITED BY THEM TOO. SHE HAS BECOME AROUSED AND SHE IS TREMBLING. CAN YOU FEEL IT?

37

44

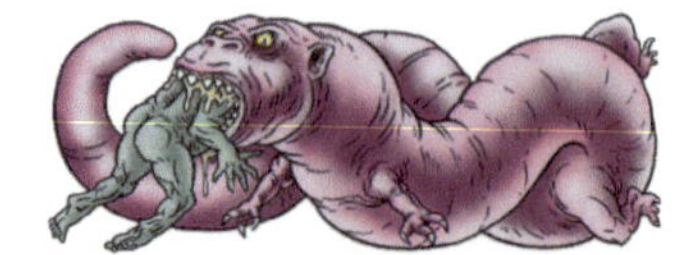

YOU CAN'T STOP NOW, MAN MEAT! WE HAVE ONLY JUST STARTED!
THE NIGHT IS YOUNG AND WE HAVE A WHOLE TRIBE FOR YOU TO SATISFY!
GREAT OKLUGU'S DESIRES BURN BRIGHTLY TONIGHT! HER JUICES HAVE BEGUN TO FLOW!
BEST WE OFFER HER A SACRIFICE — FEED HER INSATIABLE SPIRIT.
GIVE HER ONE OF OUR PIECES OF MAN MEAT THAT CAN NO LONGER RUT AND PRAY THAT IT APPEASES HER...
YES, MY PET MANLING! NOW YOU KNOW WHAT FATE AWAITS YOU IF YOU DO NOT PLEASE US!

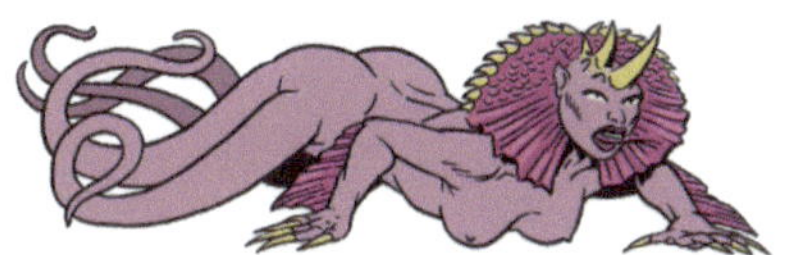

THAT VOLCANO'S RUMBLING HAS WOKEN ME...
IT HAS WOKEN US ALL, SAVAGE BITCH.
CAN'T SEE US GETTING ANY SLEEP NOW. BEST WE JUST GET TO THE BUKU BUKU VILLAGE.
DON'T LIKE THE LOOK OF THAT. COULD BLOW ANY TIME NOW, WHICH MEANS WE DON'T HAVE VERY MUCH TIME...
WHAT MAKES YOU THINK HE'LL STILL BE ALIVE WHEN WE GET THERE, BIG BITCH?
YOU WANT TO PRAY HE IS, HARD BITCH, BECAUSE WE CAN'T GO HOME WITH ONLY ONE MAN. HAVING JUST TWO IS BAD ENOUGH!
THEY WON'T KILL HIM ~ NOT IF HE CAN TAKE HARD RUTTING.
BUKU BUKU RUT THEIR CAPTIVES UNTIL THEY WASTE AWAY.
THIS ONE WILL DO! HE CAN HARDLY STAND, LET ALONE RUT...
QUICK! TAKE HIM, THROW HIM INTO OKLUGU'S HUNGRY PIT NOW!
GREAT OKLUGU WILL NOT WAIT ANY LONGER. HER GROWLING WILL TEAR THE EARTH APART!
THIS IS THE MOMENT OF THE MEANING OF YOUR MEAGRE EXISTENCE, MANLING...
ONE OF OKLUGU'S MINIONS WILL SOON DELIVER YOUR SOUL TO HER, AND THEN DEVOUR YOUR HUSK!
EVEN NOW, THEY CAN TASTE THE SCENT OF YOUR MAN MEAT ON THE NIGHT AIR!
S. CARTER T. RYYYZ ©1996
39

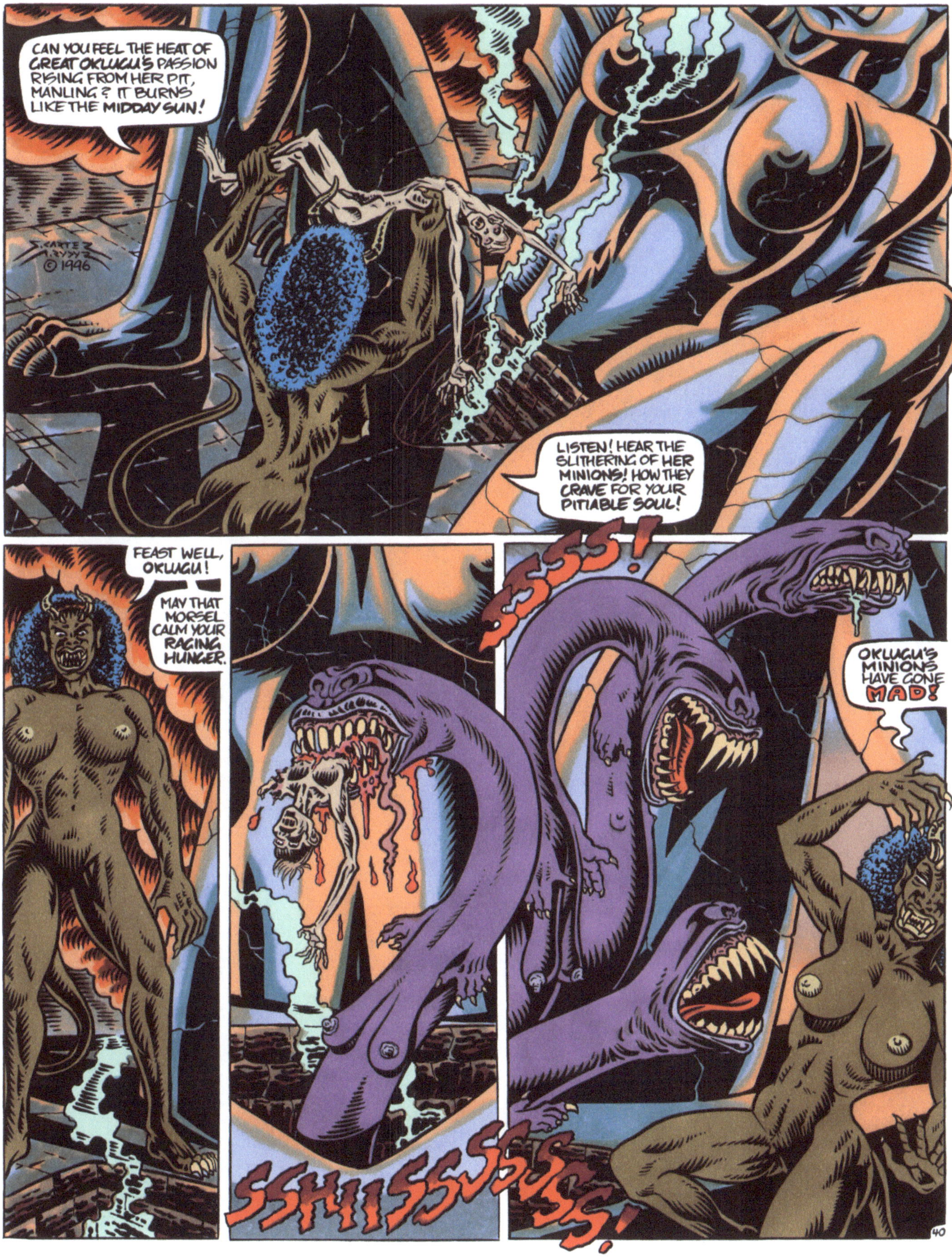

CAN YOU FEEL THE HEAT OF GREAT OKLUGU'S PASSION RISING FROM HER PIT, MANLING? IT BURNS LIKE THE MIDDAY SUN!
LISTEN! HEAR THE SLITHERING OF HER MINIONS! HOW THEY CRAVE FOR YOUR PITIABLE SOUL!
FEAST WELL, OKLUGU!
MAY THAT MORSEL CALM YOUR RAGING HUNGER.
SSSS!
OKLUGU'S MINIONS HAVE GONE MAD!
SSHIISSSSSSS!

S.CARTER
© 1996

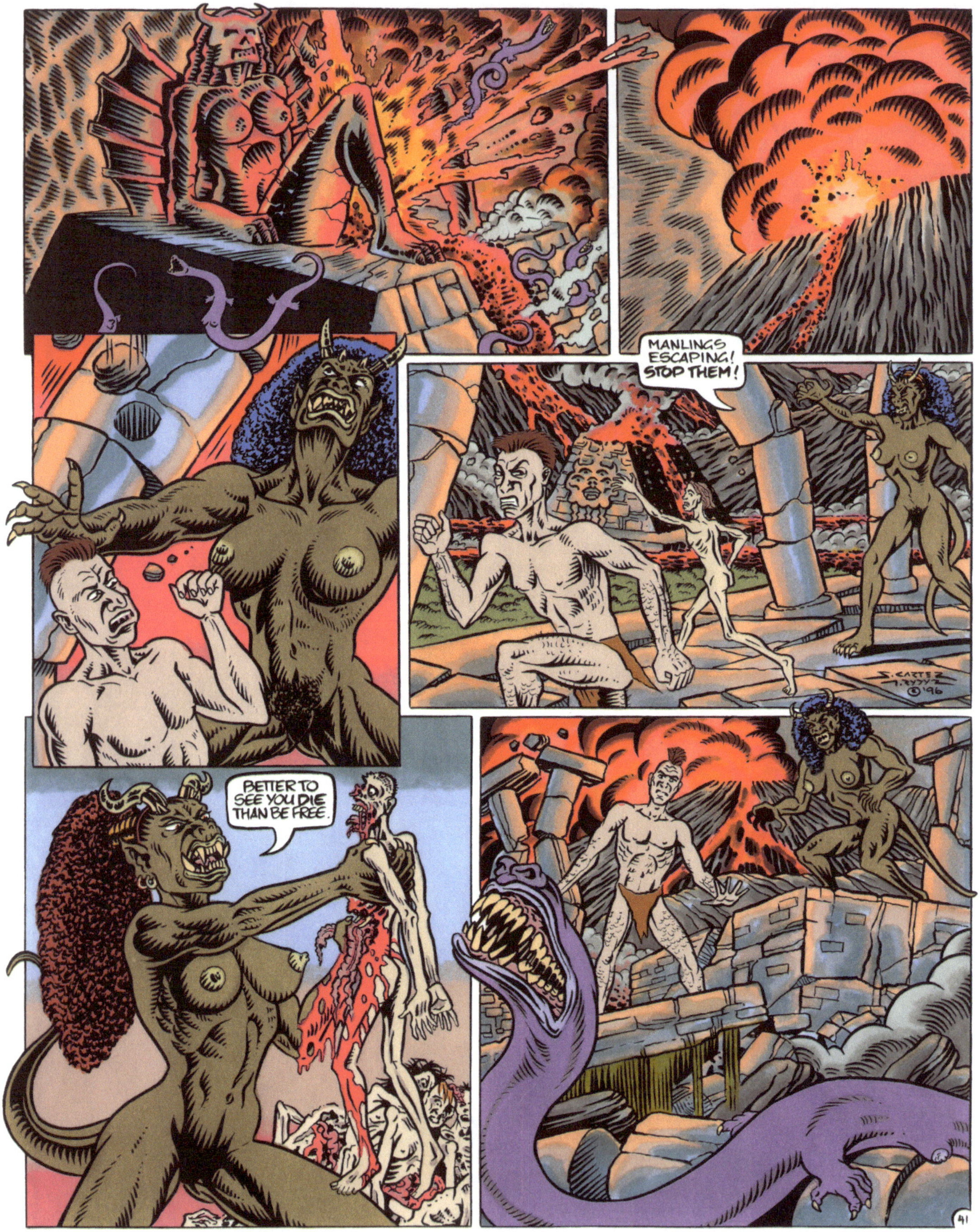

MANLINGS ESCAPING! STOP THEM!

BETTER TO SEE YOU DIE THAN BE FREE.

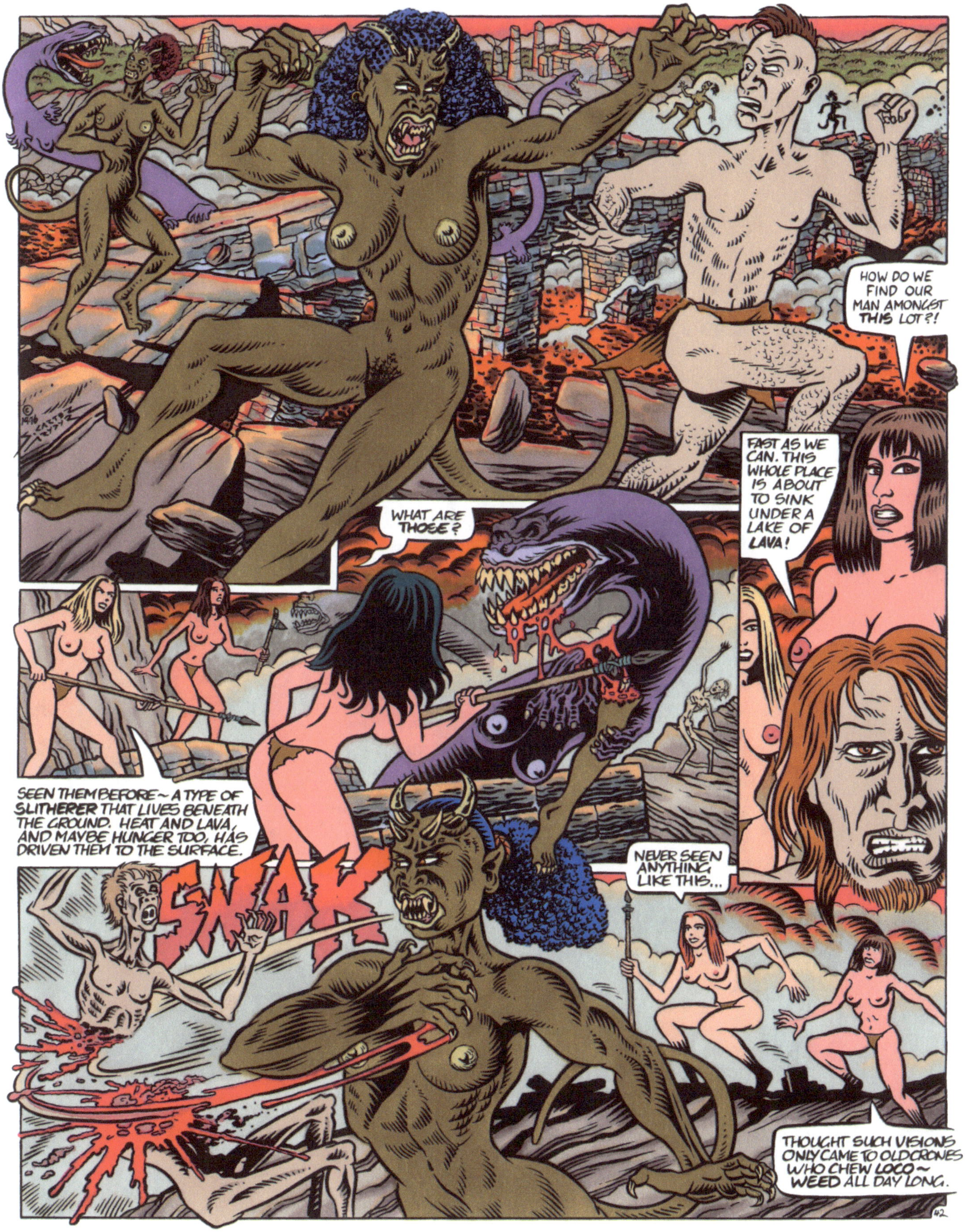

HOW DO WE FIND OUR MAN AMONGST THIS LOT?!
WHAT ARE THOSE?
FAST AS WE CAN. THIS WHOLE PLACE IS ABOUT TO SINK UNDER A LAKE OF LAVA!
SEEN THEM BEFORE~ A TYPE OF SLITHERER THAT LIVES BENEATH THE GROUND. HEAT AND LAVA, AND MAYBE HUNGER TOO, HAS DRIVEN THEM TO THE SURFACE.
NEVER SEEN ANYTHING LIKE THIS...
SNAK
THOUGHT SUCH VISIONS ONLY CAME TO OLD CRONES WHO CHEW LOCO~ WEED ALL DAY LONG.

BE EASIER TO JUST RAID ANOTHER VILLAGE FOR MEN, WOULDN'T IT? NOTHING WORTH FIGHTING FOR HERE!
YOU MAY BE RIGHT AT THAT, SAVAGE BITCH,
BUT BIG BITCH HAS A FANCY FOR THE ONE WE'VE COME HERE FOR!
WATCH YOUR MOUTH, HARD BITCH!
TASTE OF BLOOD SENDS THEM RIGHT OFF, EVEN IF IT'S THEIR OWN!
GOOD FOR US! GETS THEM OFF OUR BACKS.
THERE HE IS!
I DON'T BELIEVE IT!
THEY ACTUALLY CAME HERE AFTER ME!
S. CARTEZ
© 1996
43

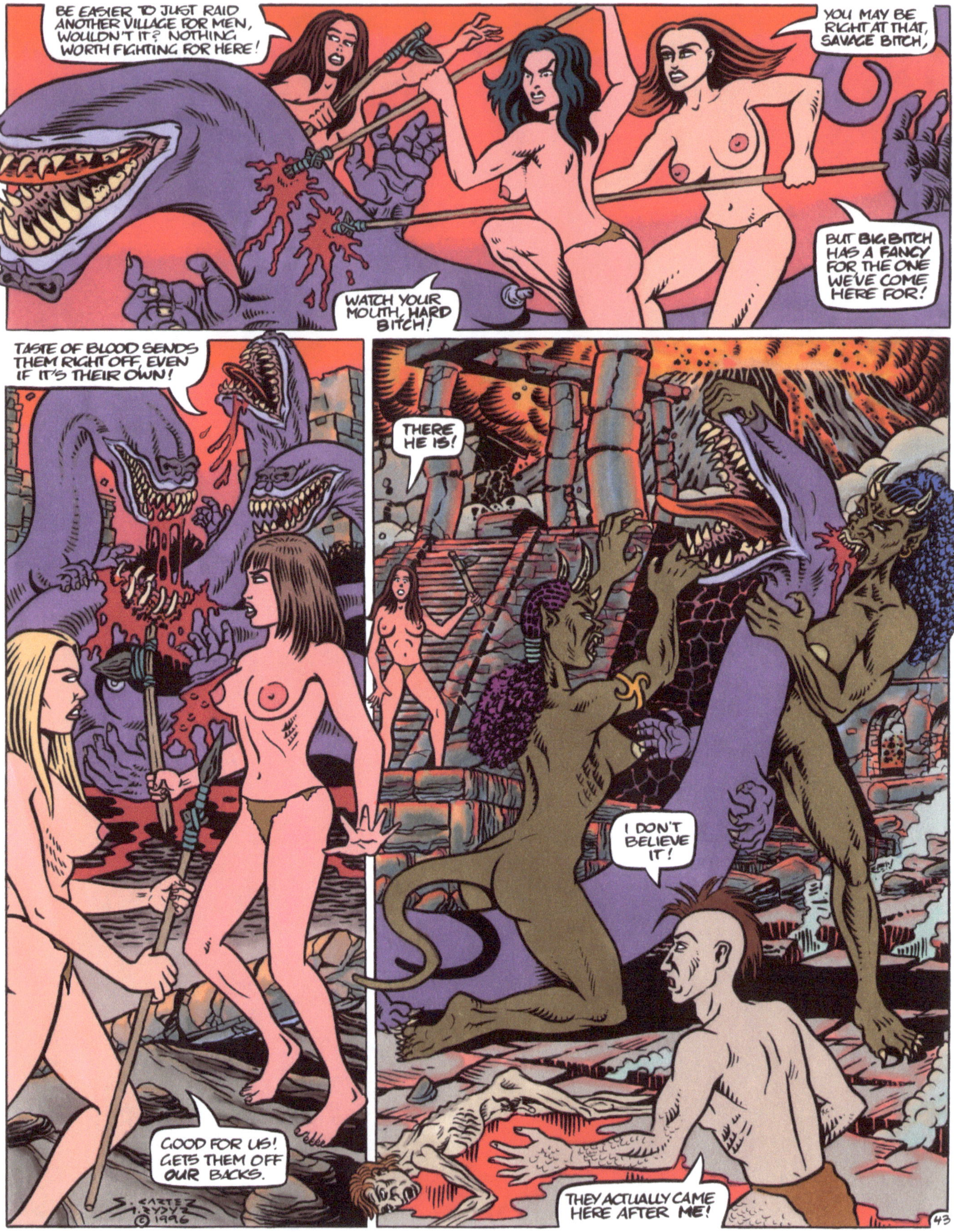

50

C'MON, THIS WAY! THREE OF THEM RIGHT BEHIND US!
NEVER THOUGHT I'D BE GLAD TO SEE YOU LOT!
JUST AS WELL YOU'RE STILL ALIVE, AFTER ALL THIS!
KRAK-KRASSH!
GOT OUT JUST IN TIME!
YOU GIRLS JUST SAVED ME FROM A FATE WORSE THAN DEATH!
AND YOU CAN SHOW YOUR GRATITUDE BY STAYING WITH US... GOT THAT?!
YOU NEED NOT WORRY.
GOT NO INTENTION OF RUNNING OFF WITH ANY STRAY HUNTING TROLLOPS, I'M YOURS.

ALL WE'VE BEEN DOING ON THIS TRIP IS FIGHTING OFF WEIRD BEASTS AND SLAVERING WOMANIMALS,
AND THEN, WHEN WE DO GET A BREAK, WE HAVE TO FIX OURSELVES NEW WEAPONS ALL THE TIME.
THIS IS THE TENTH SPEAR I'VE MADE SO FAR...
STOP COMPLAINING, SAVAGE BITCH! THIS IS THE LIFE OF A HUNTRESS!
OR WOULD YOU RATHER THE DULL EXISTENCE OF ONE OF THOSE FAT MOTHERS,
GOSSIPING ALL DAY AND ALWAYS PICKING UP AFTER THE CHILDREN?
I HAVE TO SAY, A MAN COULD DO A WHOLE LOT WORSE FOR HIMSELF THAN HAVING TO FEED THE HUNGER-CRAVED SPIRITS OF YOU GIRLS!
MAKE SURE YOU REMEMBER THAT AND BEHAVE YOURSELF REAL GOOD, AND THEN WE'LL LOOK AFTER YOU.
HOPE WE STOP SOON. BEEN AT IT ALL NIGHT. GOT TO GET ME SOME REST AND SLEEP!
NOW GET BACK TO WORK, AND NO COMPLAINING...
YEAH! ONE THING I CAN'T STAND IS A LAZY, COMPLAINING MAN WHO PRETENDS NOT TO LIKE IT!
YOU'VE DONE REALLY WELL, SAVAGE BITCH. NOT MANY GIRLS CAN HANDLE A TRIP THIS WILD ON THEIR FIRST TIME OUT AWAY FROM THE TRIBE.
THE WORST OF IT'S OVER. IT'S SMOOTH GOING ALL THE WAY, NOW. THAT'S THE FLOODPLAIN, DOWN THERE. HOME'S ONLY A FEW DAYS AWAY,
BE THERE BEFORE YOU KNOW IT...
© 1996
45

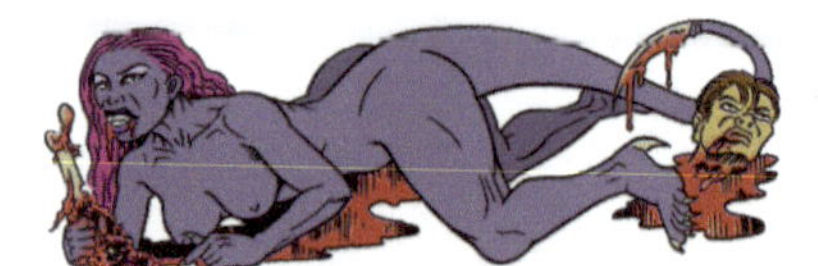

THE FURY OF BLOOD BITCH
BY STEVE CARTER & ANTOINETTE RYDYR
STARRING
SAVAGE BITCH

PART ONE
HAVOC OF THE HARPIES

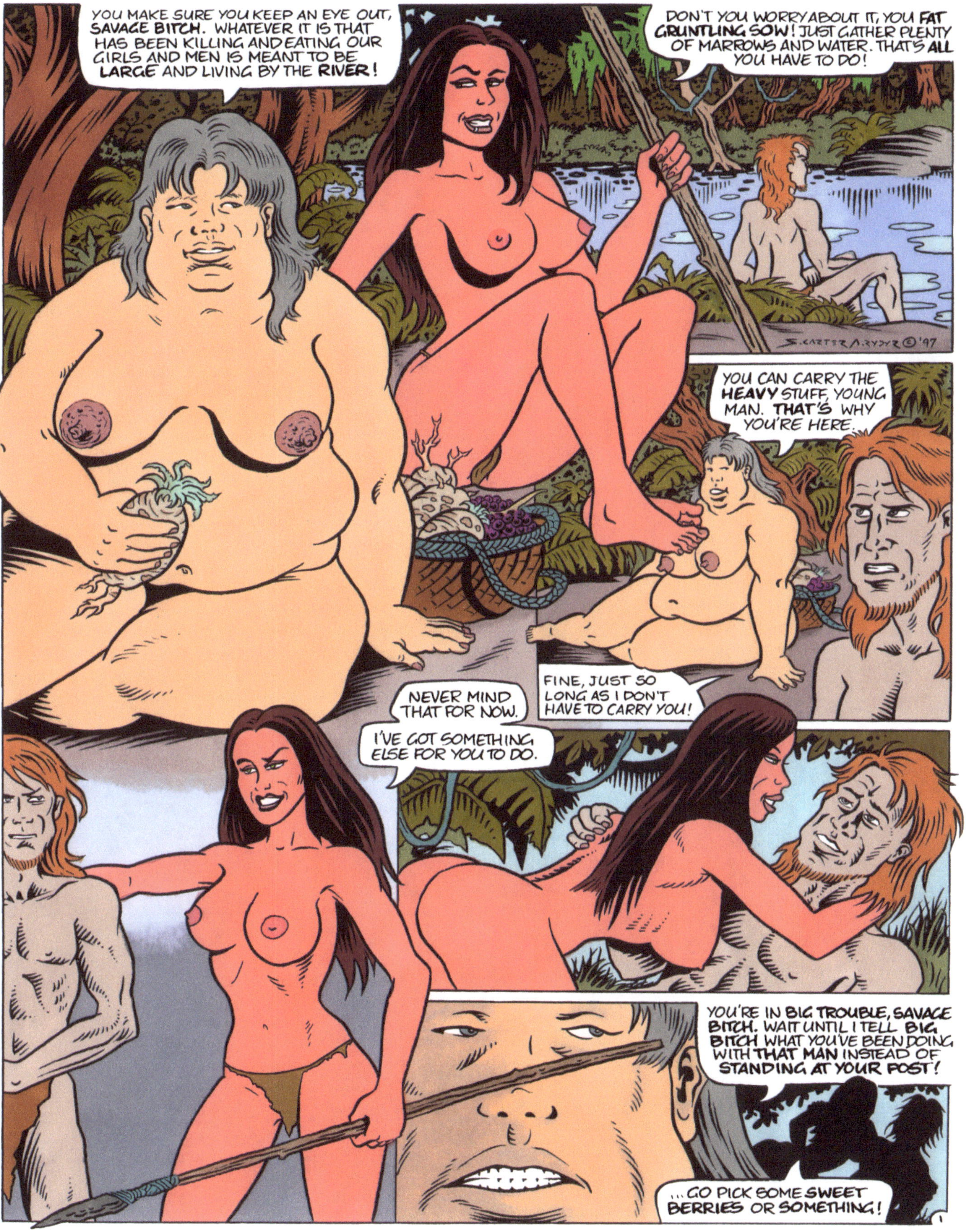

YOU MAKE SURE YOU KEEP AN EYE OUT, SAVAGE BITCH. WHATEVER IT IS THAT HAS BEEN KILLING AND EATING OUR GIRLS AND MEN IS MEANT TO BE LARGE AND LIVING BY THE RIVER!

DON'T YOU WORRY ABOUT IT, YOU FAT GRUNTLING SOW! JUST GATHER PLENTY OF MARROWS AND WATER. THAT'S ALL YOU HAVE TO DO!

YOU CAN CARRY THE HEAVY STUFF, YOUNG MAN. THAT'S WHY YOU'RE HERE.

NEVER MIND THAT FOR NOW.

I'VE GOT SOMETHING ELSE FOR YOU TO DO.

FINE, JUST SO LONG AS I DON'T HAVE TO CARRY YOU!

YOU'RE IN BIG TROUBLE, SAVAGE BITCH. WAIT UNTIL I TELL BIG BITCH WHAT YOU'VE BEEN DOING WITH THAT MAN INSTEAD OF STANDING AT YOUR POST!

...GO PICK SOME SWEET BERRIES OR SOMETHING!

HEY! GET AWAY! LEAVE ME ALONE!
THOSE SCURRIERS ARE SURE KEEPING HER BUSY.
ALWAYS WANTED TO SEE HOW A FAT MOTHER'D COPE WITH A SWARM OF MISCHIEVOUS SCURRIERS!
YOU MEAN YOU'RE NOT EVEN GOING TO HELP HER?
NO WAY! HAVEN'T HAD SO MUCH FUN IN AGES!
LOOK! THEY'VE STOPPED HARASSING HER... THEY'RE JUST STANDING THERE LIKE THEY'RE WAITING FOR SOMETHING TO HAPPEN... WHAT'S GOTTEN INTO THEM?
SOMETHING'S BOTHERING THEM. THEY'RE ACTING VERY ANXIOUS...

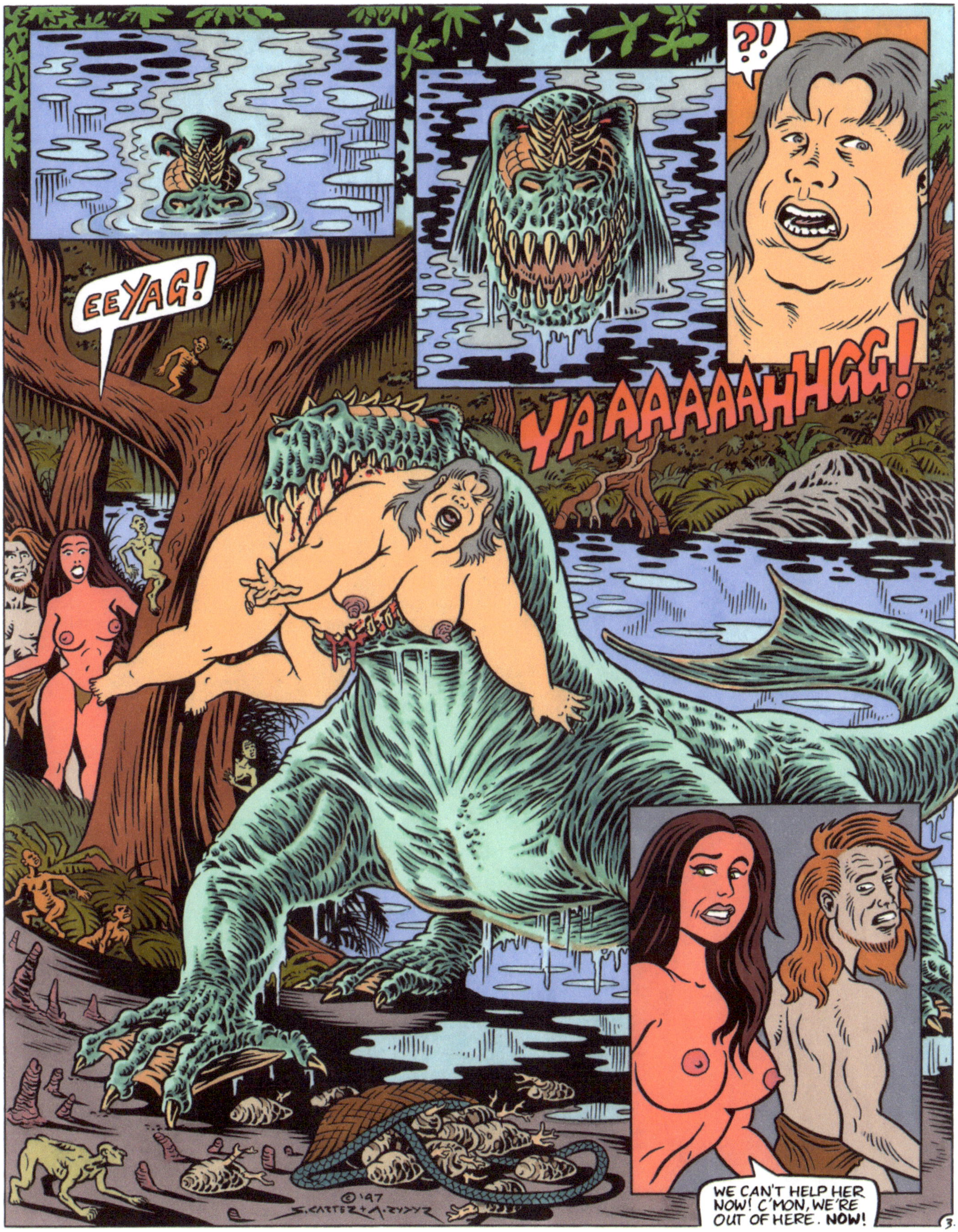

?!
EEYAG!
YAAAAAHGG!
WE CAN'T HELP HER NOW! C'MON, WE'RE OUT OF HERE. NOW!
3.

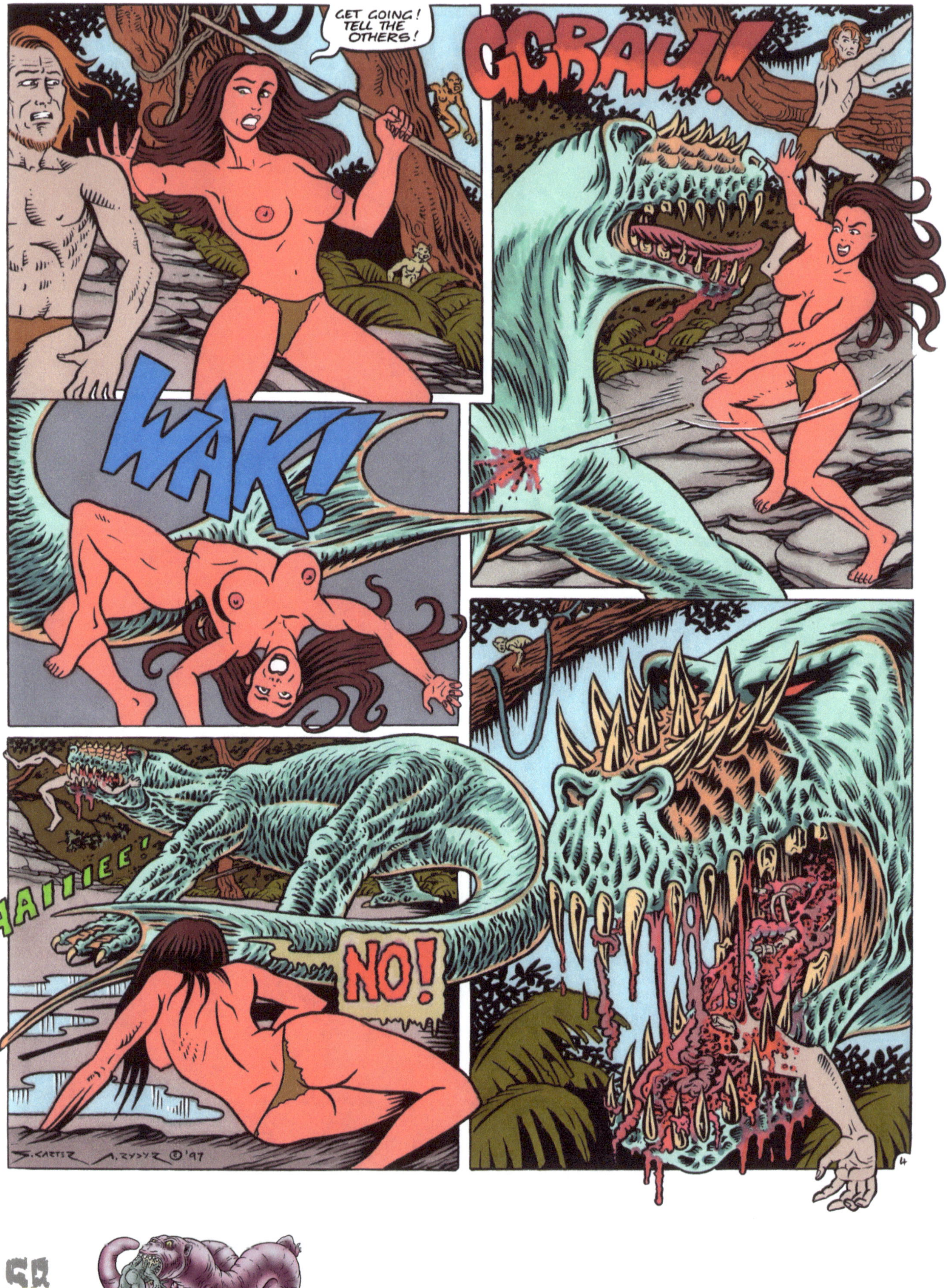

GET GOING! TELL THE OTHERS!
GGRAW!
WAK!
AAIIIEE!
NO!
58
4

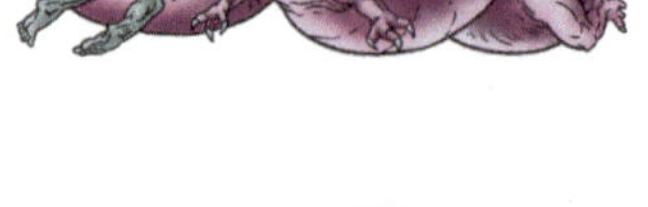

THOSE SCREAMS!
...COMING FROM THE RIVER ...WHERE SAVAGE BITCH IS!
BLOOD BITCH, HARD BITCH! ALL OF YOU! GET YOUR WEAPONS. WE'RE GOING DOWN THERE, NOW!
...LITTLE BITCH'S ALWAYS GETTING INTO TROUBLE!
DON'T JUST STARE AT IT!
KILL IT!
GGRRAAHHH!
PALE BITCH! GET BACK!
EEYAH!

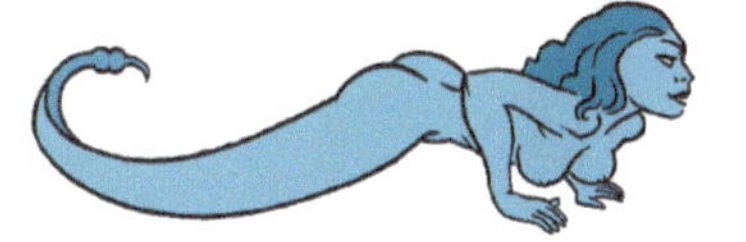

OUR SPEARS ARE ONLY MAKING IT MORE ANGRY
..., NOT WEAKER!
JUST KEEP STABBING IT, CRAZY BITCH.
IT'LL BLEED TO DEATH... EVENTUALLY.
THERE'S BIG BITCH, CRAZY BITCH AND BLOOD BITCH...
THEY'RE ALL DOWN HERE FIGHTING THE RIVER BEAST.
GOING TO HAVE TO HELP THEM!
THIS BROKEN SPEAR WILL BE OF USE...
THERE'S SAVAGE BITCH! WHERE'D SHE COME FROM?
WHAT'S SHE DOING CLIMBING UP ONTO THE THING'S BACK?
GET UP HERE...
REACH IT'S HEAD...
...BEST CHANCE OF KILLING IT!
GOT TO HOLD ON TIGHT! HIT THE EYE!

RAAUGGH!
R

K-SPLASH!

SAVAGE BITCH!
ARE YOU HURT?
GOOD FIGHTING!
IT WAS YOUR BLOW THAT KILLED IT!
© 1997
S. CARTER   A. RYDYR

NOT MUCH LEFT OF THESE TWO...
THAT'S ONE MOTHER AND ONE MAN DOWN...
SAVAGE BITCH WAS SUPPOSED TO LOOK OUT FOR THEM...
7

YOU'LL LIVE, PALE BITCH. COULD HAVE BEEN MUCH WORSE. YOU'RE LUCKY... NO ORGANS PUNCTURED, SPINE AND RIBS SOMEHOW DIDN'T GET CRUSHED OR SNAPPED...
THE OINTMENT FROM THESE LEAVES WILL DULL THE PAIN AND HELP THE HEALING PROCESS.
EEYAGH!
WHAT ABOUT HER?
SHE'S PROBABLY BETTER OFF DEAD! FOR NOW, SHE'S OUT OF IT ON THOSE BERRIES WE GAVE HER.
...CLEANED THE STUMP UP AS BEST AS WE COULD. ALL SHE'S GOT TO LOOK FORWARD TO NOW IS LIFE WITH THE FAT MOTHERS.
HER HUNTING AND FIGHTING DAYS ARE OVER.
SO YOUNG, TOO...
THE FACT IS, SAVAGE BITCH FAILED TO PROTECT A MOTHER AND ONE OF OUR MEN!
...THE PUNISHMENT FOR THAT IS BANISHMENT!
HANG ON, THEY'RE AT IT AGAIN—ARGUING ABOUT SAVAGE BITCH.
SHE ALSO FOUGHT BRAVELY, CARING NOTHING FOR HER OWN LIFE, AND FELLED THE VERY BEAST WHICH HAD BEEN HAUNTING US FOR THE WHOLE STORM SEASON!
IT IS BECAUSE OF HER COURAGE THAT NO MORE OF US WILL BE KILLED BY THE KILLER BEAST!
AND THAT IS HARDLY A REASON TO BANISH HER, BLOOD BITCH.
I DON'T THINK SHE LIKES YOU, SAVAGE BITCH.
DON'T MATTER, WILD BITCH. SHE'S JUST A RUNT-HOG RUTTER ANYHOW!
BIG BITCH IS RIGHT. BESIDES, SHE IS OUR LEADER,
AND WHAT SHE SAYS IS DONE!
SHUT YOUR MOUTH, CRAZY BITCH! THIS IS NOT OVER, YET!
© 1997 S. CARTER A. RYDER
8

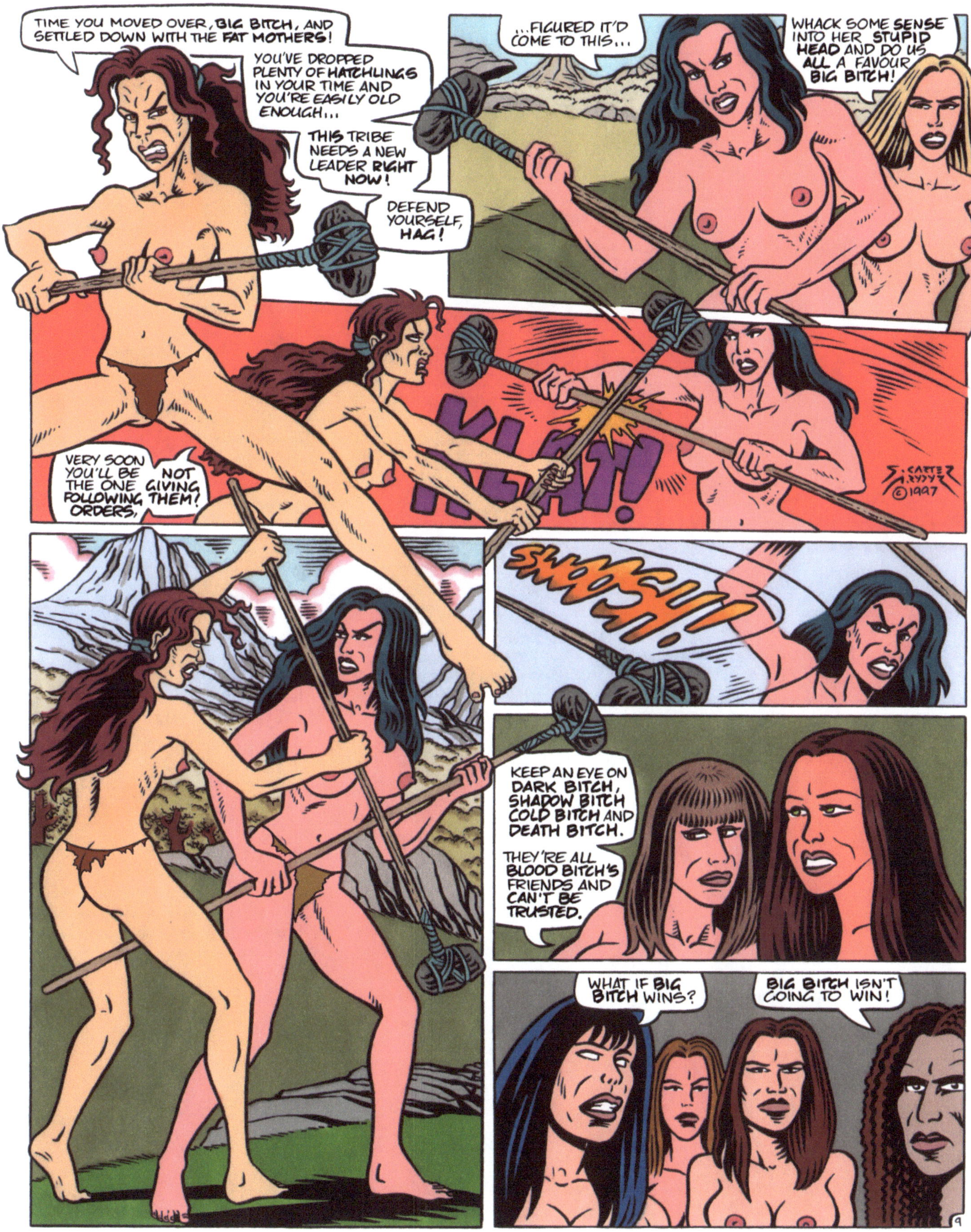

TIME YOU MOVED OVER, BIG BITCH, AND SETTLED DOWN WITH THE FAT MOTHERS!
YOU'VE DROPPED PLENTY OF HATCHLINGS IN YOUR TIME AND YOU'RE EASILY OLD ENOUGH...
THIS TRIBE NEEDS A NEW LEADER RIGHT NOW!
DEFEND YOURSELF, HAG!
...FIGURED IT'D COME TO THIS...
WHACK SOME SENSE INTO HER STUPID HEAD AND DO US ALL A FAVOUR BIG BITCH!
KLAK!
S. CARTER
© 1997
VERY SOON YOU'LL BE THE ONE GIVING ORDERS, NOT FOLLOWING THEM!
SHOOSH!
KEEP AN EYE ON DARK BITCH, SHADOW BITCH, COLD BITCH AND DEATH BITCH.
THEY'RE ALL BLOOD BITCH'S FRIENDS AND CAN'T BE TRUSTED.
WHAT IF BIG BITCH WINS?
BIG BITCH ISN'T GOING TO WIN!
9

SUGHH!
BLOOD BITCH NEEDS HELP! ...HOPED IT WOULDN'T GO THIS WAY...
LOOKS LIKE WE'RE GOING TO DO IT THE HARD WAY, DEATH BITCH. GO FOR IT- WE'LL BE RIGHT BEHIND YOU.
SHOULD HAVE KNOWN THEY'D TRY SOMETHING LIKE THIS!
GOT TO STOP THE MAD BITCH!
BITCH!
?!
UUGH!
TREACHEROUS BITCH TRIED TO STAB BIG BITCH IN THE BACK!
YOU SHOULD BE PUT TO DEATH, SLAG!
NO!
THING IS, YOU SCRAGS HAVE BEEN RUNNING THIS TRIBE FOR TOO LONG!
NOBODY HERE CARES WHAT YOU THINK, CRAZY BITCH BECAUSE YOU'RE CRAZY ANYWAY! YOU ALL ARE!
...TIME THE WHOLE BUNCH OF YOU GOT OUT! AND TAKE THAT VILE LITTLE SLAG, SAVAGE BITCH, WITH YOU!

10

YOU IGNORANT SLAGS WANT TO GET RID OF ME? YOU'RE WELCOME TO TRY, ANYTIME!
LET'S SMASH THEIR ROTTEN HEADS IN!
WE'RE WITH YOU, BIG BITCH!
LOOK AT THIS! THE BIG FIVE PUSHY BITCHES! ALL LINED UP READY TO TELL US WHAT TO DO YET AGAIN...
NOT THIS TIME, BITCHES! NO ONE WANTS YOU HERE. EVERYONE IS SICK TO DEATH OF YOUR STUPID WAYS! EVEN THE FAT MOTHERS CAN'T STAND YOU ANY MORE!
OH, MY! THIS IS TERRIBLE! OUR TRIBE'S SPLITTING APART!
WHAT ARE YOU BABBLING ABOUT, PALE BITCH?
THIS HAS BEEN A LONG TIME COMING!
...BEEN WAITING FOR THIS DAY!
YEAH! I'D BEEN WONDERING WHEN BLOOD BITCH AND HER FRIENDS'D FINALLY GET UP THE NERVE TO ACTUALLY DO SOMETHIN'.
©1997
S. CARTER

APPEARS BLOOD BITCH AND THE GIRLS NEED A HAND TO GET RID OF THE VERMIN!
I GO WHERE BIG BITCH GOES. NO POINT STAYIN' HERE...
ONE PACK OF BITCHES IS THE SAME AS ANOTHER ...WON'T BE ANY WORSE OFF IF YOU STAY.
NO WAY! I DON'T WANT BLOOD BITCH RUNNIN' MY LIFE!
G'WAN! OFF WITH YOU!
GO AWAY AND DON'T COME BACK!
...WATCH IT, YOU HIDEOUS FAT SOW!
HEY! WHERE D'YOU THINK YOU'RE GOING? YOU CAN'T GO WITH THEM! GET BACK HERE NOW!
LET'S GO, GIRLS! THIS TRIBE'S FULL OF LOSERS AND FOOLS...
NO WAY I'M STAYIN' WITH A PACK OF FAT BLOATED TROLLOPS!
BESIDES, I OWE BIG BITCH FOR SAVING MY LIFE.

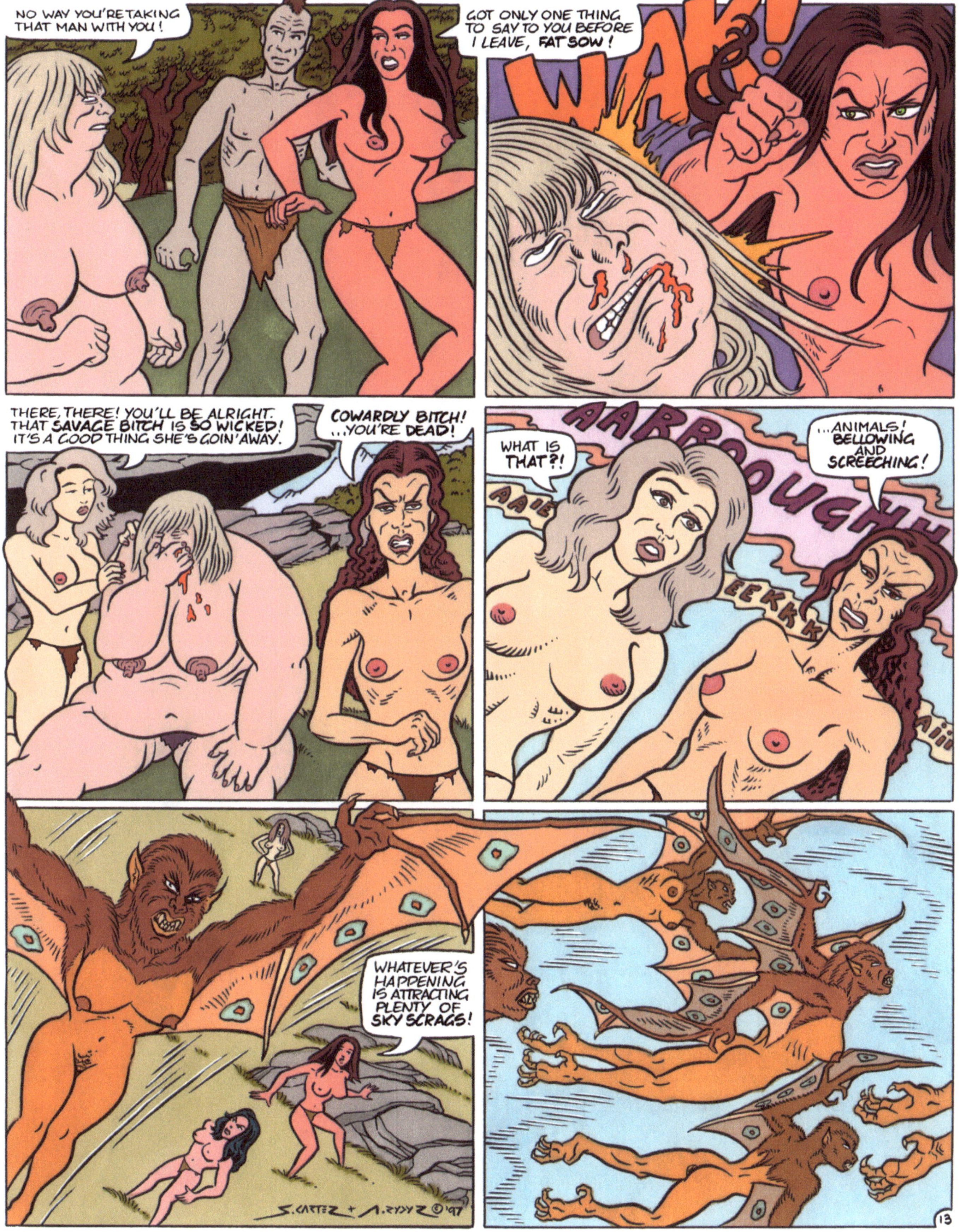

NO WAY YOU'RE TAKING THAT MAN WITH YOU!
GOT ONLY ONE THING TO SAY TO YOU BEFORE I LEAVE, FAT SOW!
WAK!
THERE, THERE! YOU'LL BE ALRIGHT. THAT SAVAGE BITCH IS SO WICKED! IT'S A GOOD THING SHE'S GOIN' AWAY.
COWARDLY BITCH! ...YOU'RE DEAD!
WHAT IS THAT?!
AARROOUGHH
AAIE
EEKKK
AIIE
...ANIMALS! BELLOWING AND SCREECHING!
WHATEVER'S HAPPENING IS ATTRACTING PLENTY OF SKY SCRAGS!
S. CARTER + A. RYDY © '97
13

GRASSLANDS STOMPERS...! CRAZED AND STAMPEDING!

SKY SCRAGS ARE DRIVING THEM WILD!

SKRAAH!
AAARROOO OUGH!
AGH!
GET UP HERE, OUT OF THE WAY!
WHAT ABOUT SAVAGE BITCH AND THEM...?
WE'LL DEAL WITH THEM LATER...

RIGHT NOW IS A GOOD TIME TO LEAVE...
GRAB HOLD OF ANY WEAPONS YOU CAN AND GET MOVING!

SK
SKRARKEE!!
THERE'S SKY SCRAGS EVERYWHERE! WHAT'S GOING ON?
...AT LEAST TWO DIFFERENT BREEDS OF THEM! AND THE NOISE! IT'S ENOUGH TO SCARE THE DEAD! WHY DO SKY SCRAGS HAVE SUCH WRETCHED VOICES?
LOOK! THEY'RE FIGHTING.
MAYBE IT'S A SKY SCRAG WAR!
SUCH MAD FURY! IT'S AWESOME!
PRETTY SOON THEIR ATTENTION'S GOING TO FALL ON US, THEN THE TROUBLE WILL REALLY START!
... UNLESS WE MOVE OFF THIS INSTANT!

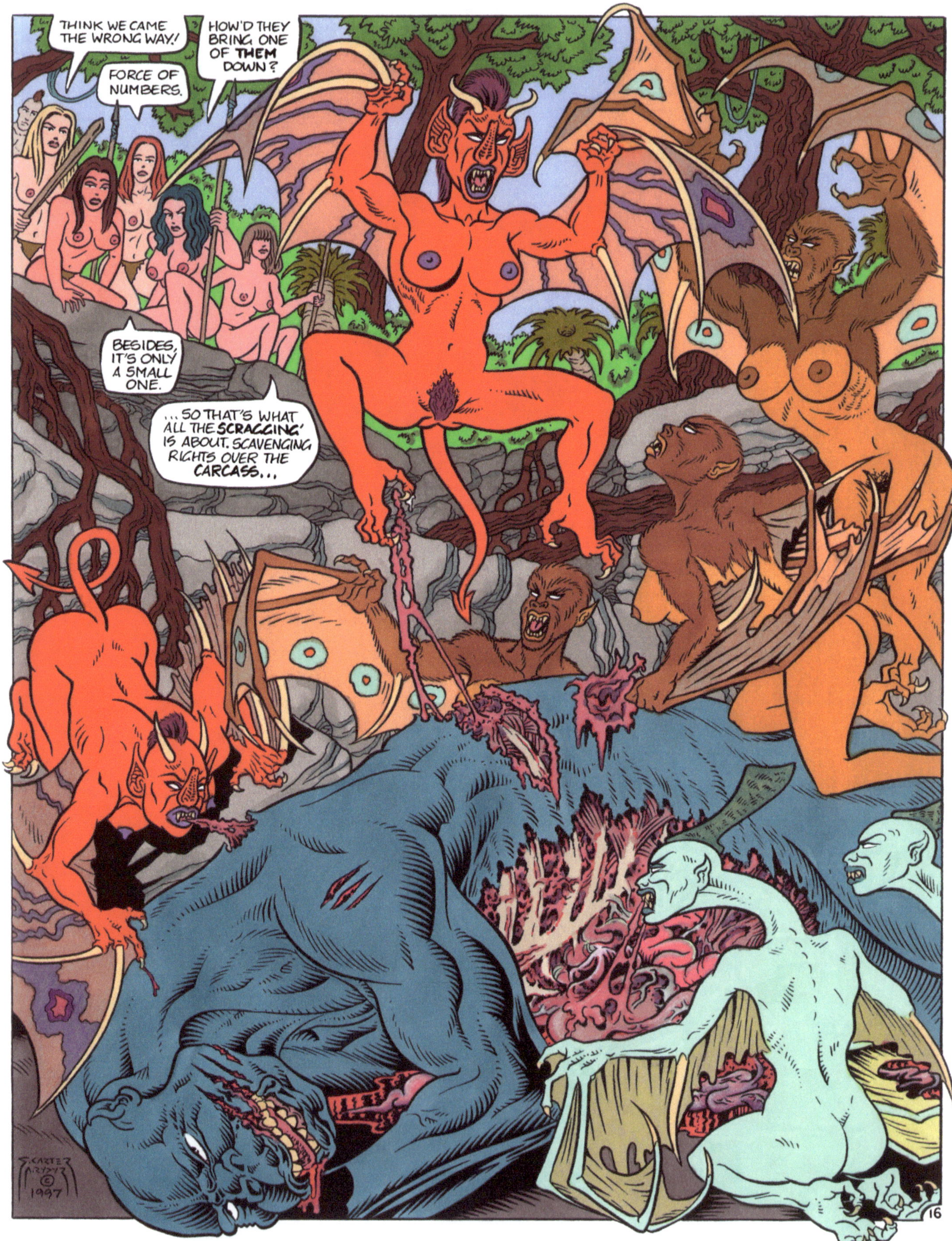

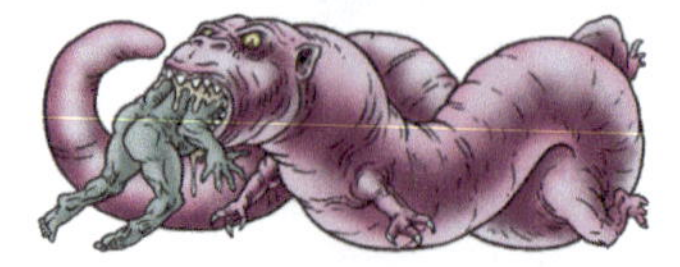

THINK WE CAME THE WRONG WAY!
HOW'D THEY BRING ONE OF THEM DOWN?
FORCE OF NUMBERS.
BESIDES, IT'S ONLY A SMALL ONE.
...SO THAT'S WHAT ALL THE SCRAGGIN' IS ABOUT. SCAVENGING RIGHTS OVER THE CARCASS...
16

THEY'VE SEEN US!
TOO MANY TO FIGHT. LET'S GO!

GET IN AMONGST THE TREES...
IT'LL BE HARDER FOR THEM TO GET AT US...
RHAHRGH!
SKRAJEEK!
©1997 S. CARTER

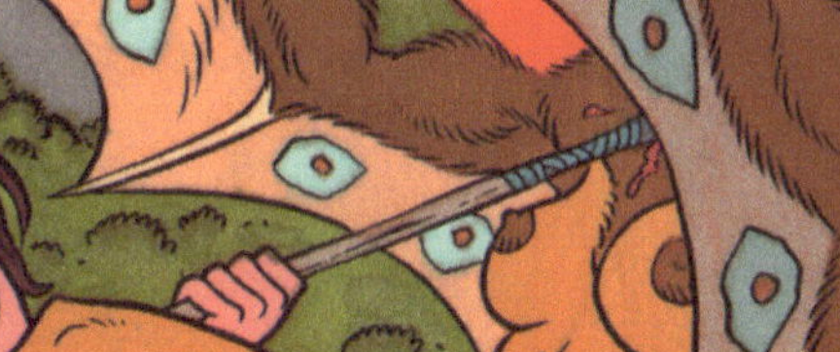

...THEY'RE EVERYWHERE! AND SO MANY DIFFERENT BREEDS, TOO!
CARTER © 1997

WATCH OUT! THEY LIKE TO SNATCH UP MEN!
?!

WHY? A MAN'S FLESH IS NO BETTER THAN ANY OTHER!
EATING FLESH IS NOT ALL THEY WANT, SAVAGE BITCH.

THE MALES OF MANY SKY SCRAG BREEDS LOOK LIKE OUR OWN.
AND RUTTING IS HOW THE ADULT FEMALES DISPLAY DOMINANCE.
THE MORE MALES A SKY SCRAG CLAIMS THE HIGHER HER RANK IN THE FLOCK!

ALSO, RUTTING STIMULATES WING-GROWTH IN THE YOUNG FEMALES. THAT'S HOW THEY BECOME ADULTS...
BUT THE MALES NEVER DEVELOP ANY WINGS...
18

SO HOW COME YOU KNOW SO MUCH ABOUT IT, HARD BITCH?
LEARNED IT OFF THE CRONE. REMEMBER HER?
...AN INFORMED HUNTRESS IS ONE WHO WILL SURVIVE!
BESIDES, IT ALL FASCINATES ME.

QUICK! GET DOWN UNDER HERE!
©1997
S. CARTER, M. RYDYR

...GONE BACK TO FIGHTING ONE ANOTHER, FOR NOW...
WHEN IS IT GONNA END?
DON'T KNOW, BUT IT LOOKS LIKE WE'LL BE SPENDING THE NIGHT HERE.
...AT LEAST TWO WILL HAVE TO KEEP WATCH AT ALL TIMES... WE'LL TAKE IT IN TURNS.
19

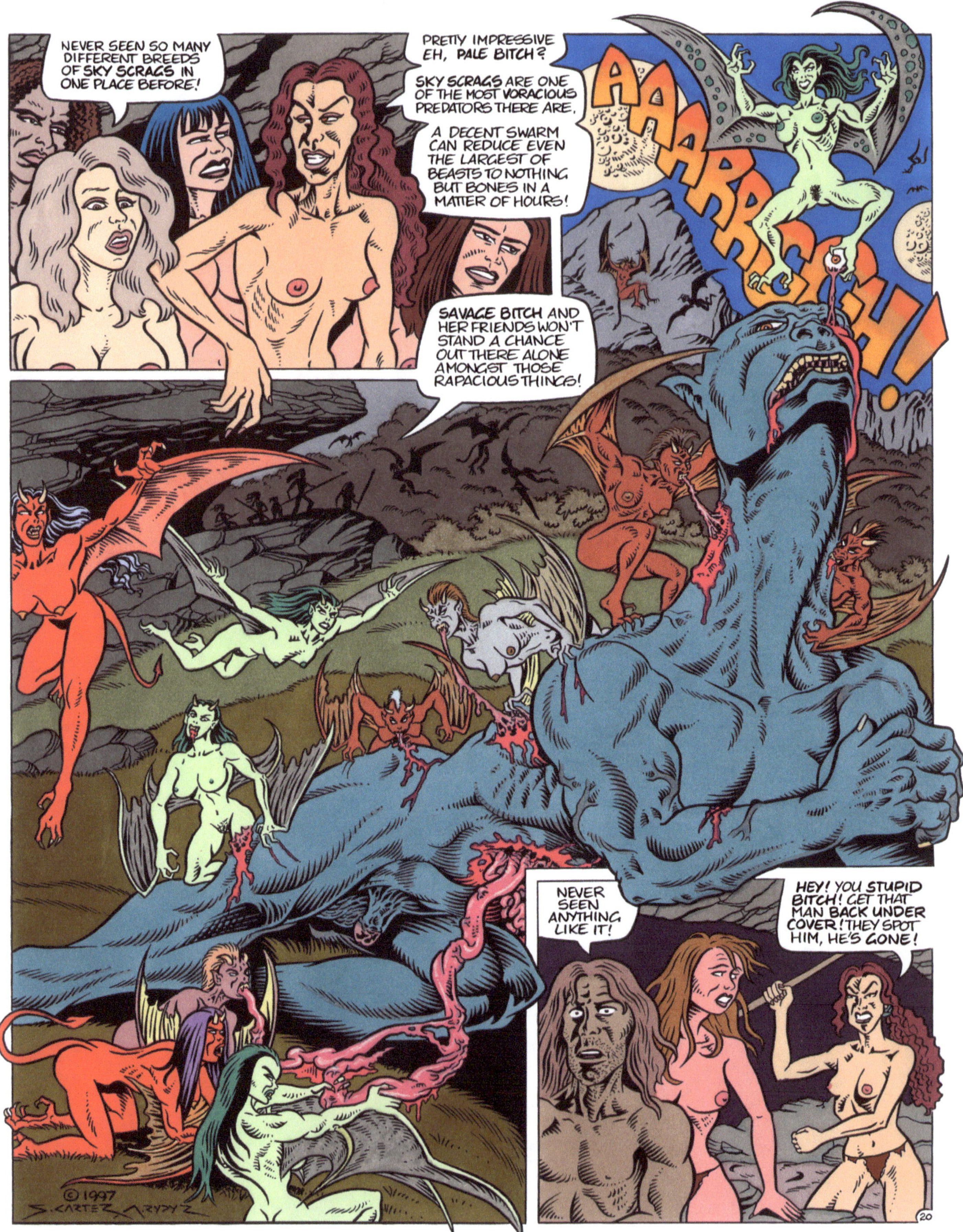

NEVER SEEN SO MANY DIFFERENT BREEDS OF SKY SCRAGS IN ONE PLACE BEFORE!
PRETTY IMPRESSIVE EH, PALE BITCH?
SKY SCRAGS ARE ONE OF THE MOST VORACIOUS PREDATORS THERE ARE,
A DECENT SWARM CAN REDUCE EVEN THE LARGEST OF BEASTS TO NOTHING BUT BONES IN A MATTER OF HOURS!
SAVAGE BITCH AND HER FRIENDS WON'T STAND A CHANCE OUT THERE ALONE AMONGST THOSE RAPACIOUS THINGS!
AAARRGGH!
NEVER SEEN ANYTHING LIKE IT!
HEY! YOU STUPID BITCH! GET THAT MAN BACK UNDER COVER! THEY SPOT HIM, HE'S GONE!
© 1997
S. CARTER ARPP'Z
20

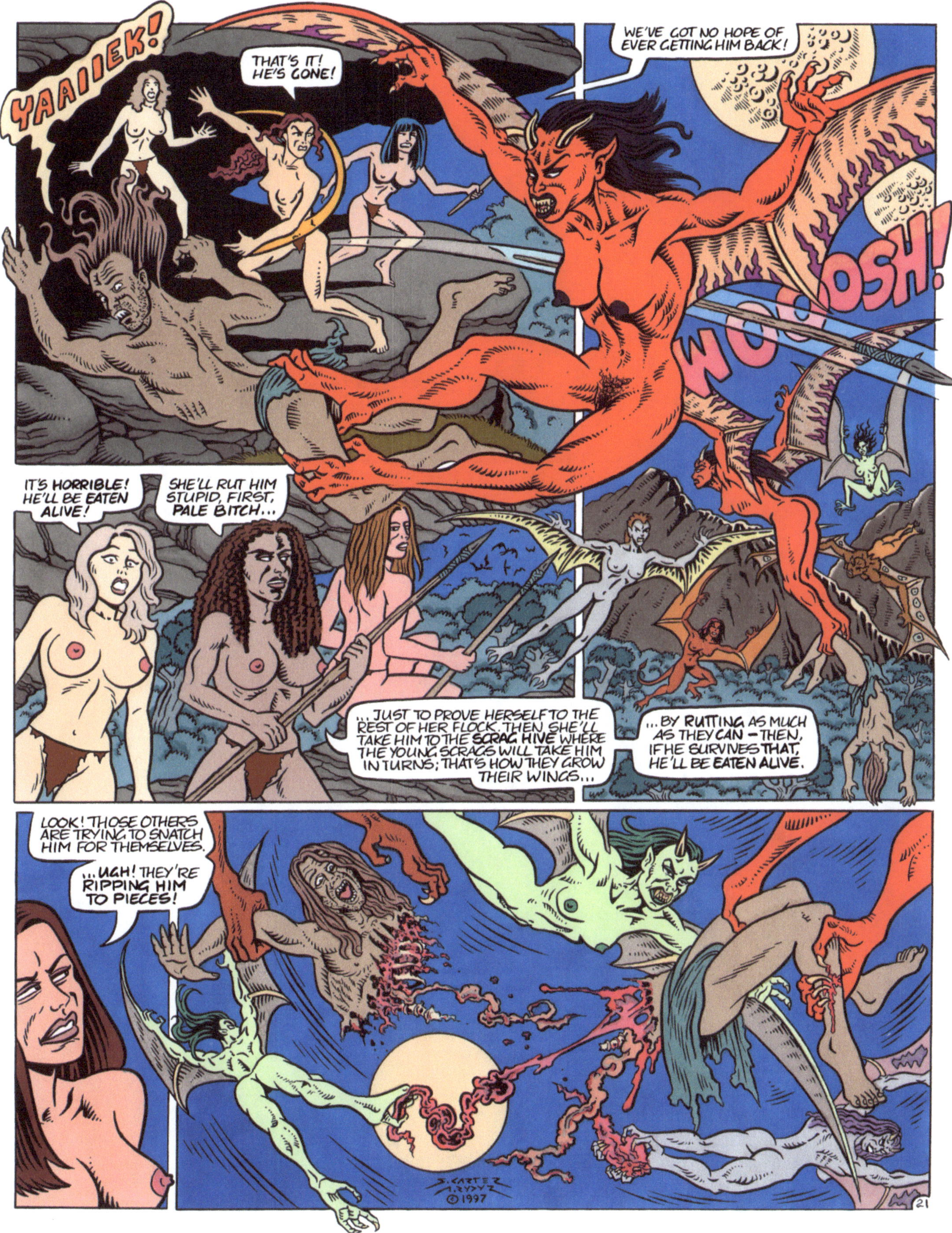

YAAIIEK!
THAT'S IT! HE'S GONE!
WE'VE GOT NO HOPE OF EVER GETTING HIM BACK!
WOOOSH!
IT'S HORRIBLE! HE'LL BE EATEN ALIVE!
SHE'LL RUT HIM STUPID, FIRST, PALE BITCH...
...JUST TO PROVE HERSELF TO THE REST OF HER FLOCK. THEN SHE'LL TAKE HIM TO THE SCRAG HIVE WHERE THE YOUNG SCRAGS WILL TAKE HIM IN TURNS; THAT'S HOW THEY GROW THEIR WINGS...
...BY RUTTING AS MUCH AS THEY CAN — THEN, IF HE SURVIVES THAT, HE'LL BE EATEN ALIVE.
LOOK! THOSE OTHERS ARE TRYING TO SNATCH HIM FOR THEMSELVES.
...UGH! THEY'RE RIPPING HIM TO PIECES!
S. CARTER T. RYDYZ © 1997
21

RRRRRR!
NOTHING MUCH LEFT BUT CARCASSES AND MEAN-LOOKING LITTLE SCAVENGERS...
COULD DO WITH A GOOD FEED. HAVEN'T EATEN SINCE THIS WHOLE THING STARTED.
DON'T THINK THOSE VICIOUS LITTLE BRUTES HAVE ANY INTENTION OF SHARING THAT CARCASS...
THEY CAN KEEP IT! NO WAY I'LL SETTLE WITH DEAD SCRAG MEAT!
S.CARTER ARTIST © 1997
THAT PLANT-EATING VARIETY OVER THERE IS MORE LIKE WHAT WE'RE AFTER...
ONE OF THOSE WILL DO NICELY.
GRiiEK!
SHLKT!

I SEE YOU HAVEN'T TAKEN YOUR TURN WITH THE MAN... THAT'S NOT LIKE YOU, SAVAGE BITCH...
DON'T THINK YOU NEED REMINDING HOW IMPORTANT IT IS TO FEED YOUR SPIRIT AS WELL AS YOUR BELLY. IT'S ESSENTIAL IF YOU WANT TO REMAIN HEALTHY IN BOTH BODY AND MIND.
I KNOW, AND I HAVE A CRAVING FOR IT AS WELL, BUT I DON'T WANT TO END UP POPPING ANY HATCHLINGS...
AFTER ALL, WASN'T IT YOU, HARD BITCH, WHO SAID THAT OVER INDULGING YOURSELF WITH THE MENFOLK CAN TURN YOU INTO A FAT MOTHER BEFORE YOUR TIME? THAT THOUGHT SCARES ME MORE THAN ANYTHING!
I'VE POPPED MORE HATCHLINGS THAN ANYONE I KNOW AND I'M TWICE AS OLD AS ANY OF YOU. HAVE I TURNED INTO A FAT MOTHER YET? DEPENDS ON HOW WELL YOU TAKE CARE OF YOURSELF.
YOU KEEP FIT, IT WON'T MATTER HOW MANY MEN YOU HAVE OR HATCHLINGS YOU DROP.
BUT YOU MUST NOT STARVE YOUR SPIRIT OR YOU'LL BECOME LAME IN THE MIND AND DESPERATE AND TWISTED, LIKE A SKY SCRAG!
WE'LL STOP HERE AND EAT THAT THING RIGHT NOW. BEST WE GET SOME FOOD IN OUR BELLIES.
LIFE'D BE SO MUCH EASIER IF OUR MEAT COULDN'T RUN FAST OR FIGHT BACK.
THAT IT WOULD, BUT THEN, EVEN THE MOST INEPT IDIOT WOULD FIND IT A SIMPLE MATTER TO SURVIVE AND THE WORLD WOULD SOON BE OVER-RUN BY CRETINS, WILD BITCH.
S. CARTER ©1997
23

PART TWO
CANYON OF DOOM

LOOK! IT'S SO BRIGHT AND MOVING STRANGELY SLOW...
THIS IS A SIGN FOR US!
THE WAY WE MUST TRAVEL HAS JUST BEEN SHOWN. OUR DESTINY LIES NORTHWARD. SOMEWHERE OUT THERE WE WILL START A NEW TRIBE AND LEAVE THE TREACHERY AND TRAUMA OF THAT SCHEMING SLAG BLOOD BITCH BEHIND US.
WHAT PLANET IS THIS?
© 1997 S. CARTER A. ?Y?Y Z
NEMESIS.
ALL WE KNOW OF IT IS THAT IT IS INHABITED BY SAVAGE AND PRIMITIVE TRIBES-WOMEN AND A VAST MENAGERIE OF DANGEROUS HUMANLIKE ANIMAL SPECIES.
COULD HAVE BEEN WORSE. AT LEAST THIS IS A HABITABLE PLANET.
WE'RE STUCK HERE NOW. THE CRAFT IS INOPERABLE AND WE'RE WAY OFF ANY KNOWN SPACE LANES!
NOBODY'S GONNA FIND US ON THIS ACCURSED OUTWORLD.
CRIKEY! IT'S A REAL TROPICAL HEAT-WAVE OUT HERE!
AND YOU CAN BET WE'LL BE SLAUGHTERED BY HOSTILE NATIVES OR RAVENOUS PREDATORS LONG BEFORE WE STARVE TO DEATH!
QUIT FLAPPIN' YER GUMS YER GROWLIN' OL' GIT, BEFORE I GIT DEPRESSED!
24

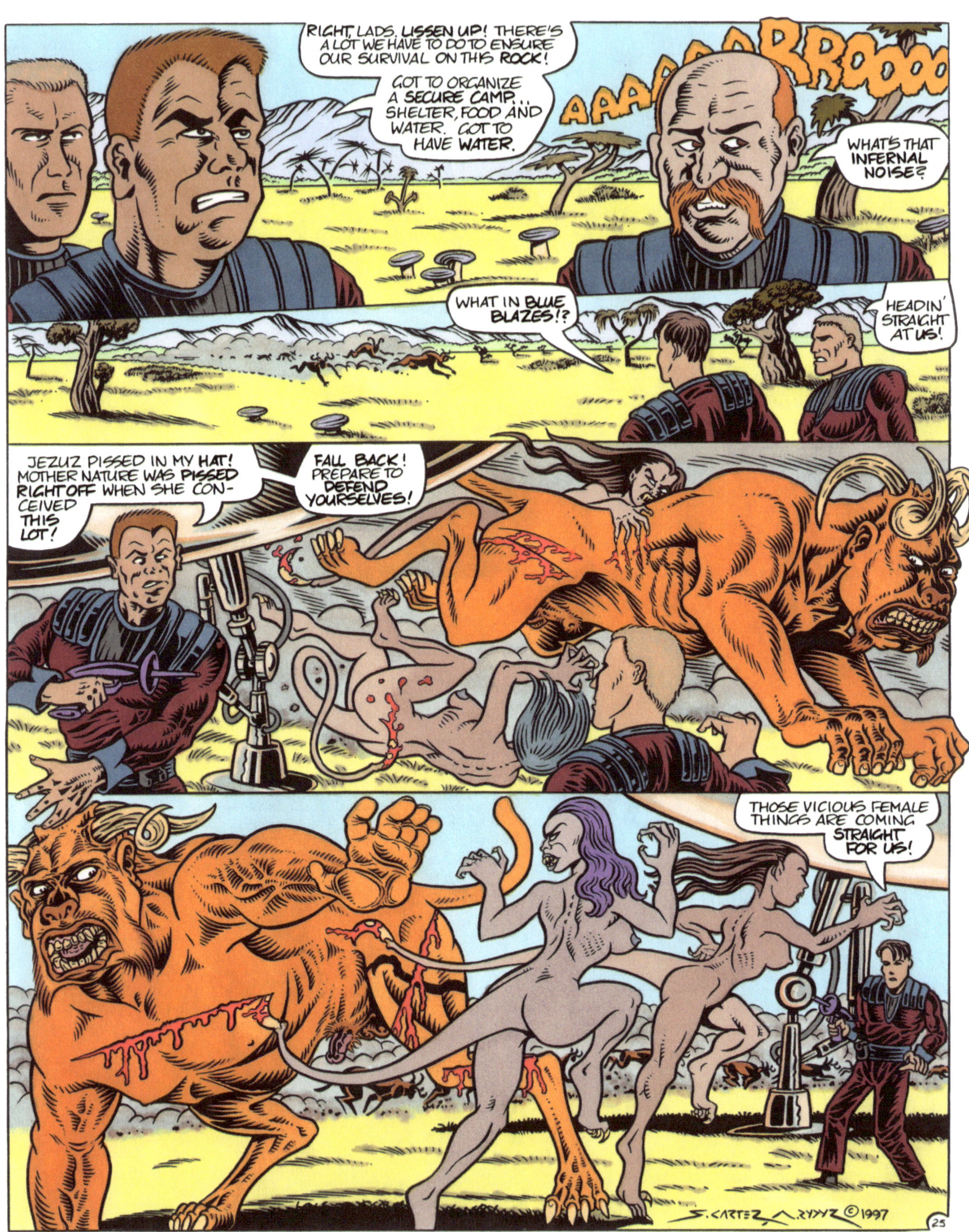

RIGHT, LADS, LISSEN UP! THERE'S A LOT WE HAVE TO DO TO ENSURE OUR SURVIVAL ON THIS ROCK!
GOT TO ORGANIZE A SECURE CAMP... SHELTER, FOOD AND WATER. GOT TO HAVE WATER.
AAAAAARRROOOO
WHAT'S THAT INFERNAL NOISE?
WHAT IN BLUE BLAZES!?
HEADIN' STRAIGHT AT US!
JEZUZ PISSED IN MY HAT! MOTHER NATURE WAS PISSED RIGHT OFF WHEN SHE CONCEIVED THIS LOT!
FALL BACK! PREPARE TO DEFEND YOURSELVES!
THOSE VICIOUS FEMALE THINGS ARE COMING STRAIGHT FOR US!
S. CARTER RYPYZ ©1997
25

VZZT!
AAARRK!! HI HEEEGH!
ZZYT!

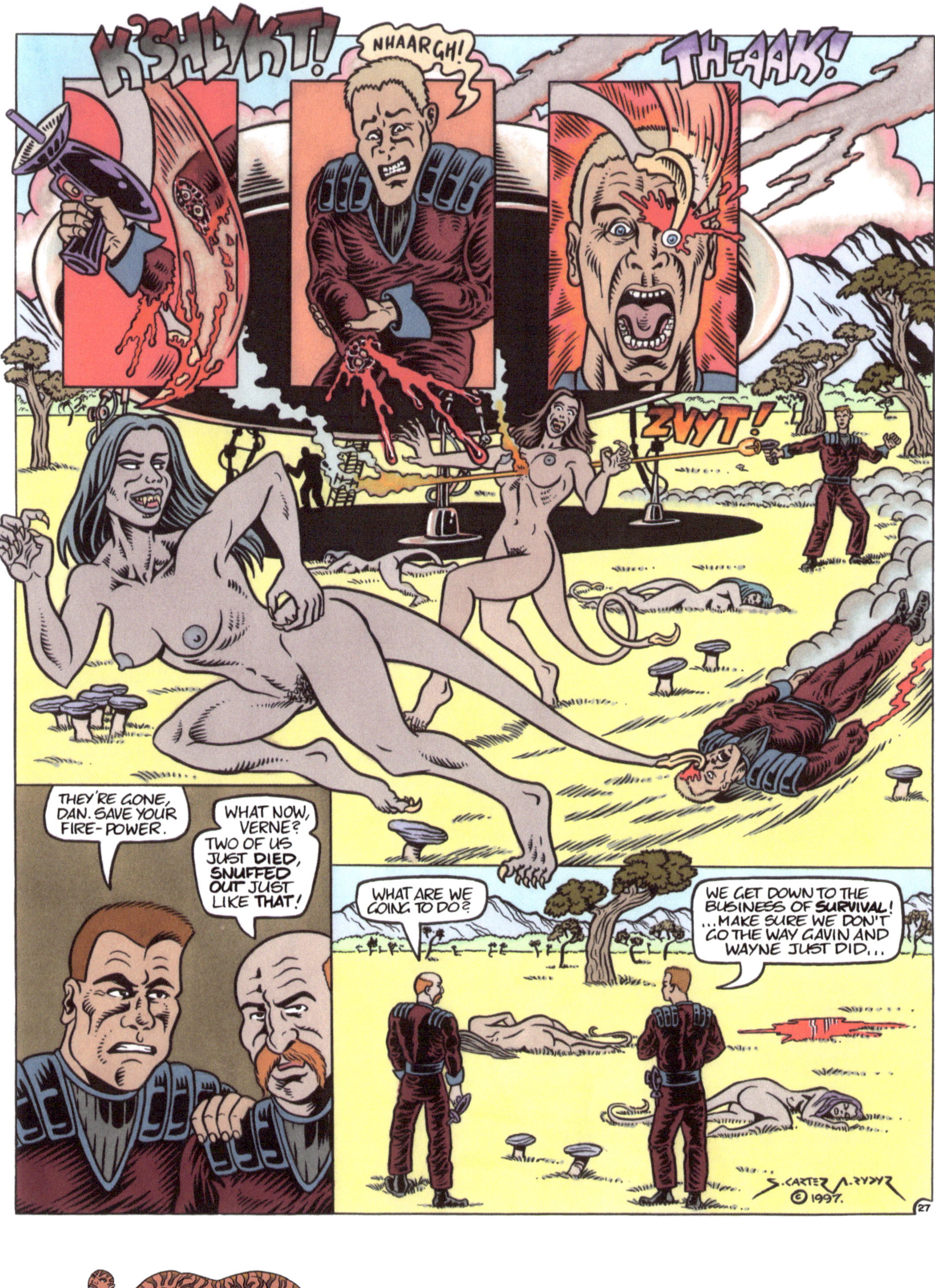

K'SHLYKT!
NHAARGH!
TH-AAK!
ZVYT!
THEY'RE GONE, DAN. SAVE YOUR FIRE-POWER.
WHAT NOW, VERNE? TWO OF US JUST DIED, SNUFFED OUT JUST LIKE THAT!
WHAT ARE WE GOING TO DO?
WE GET DOWN TO THE BUSINESS OF SURVIVAL! ...MAKE SURE WE DON'T GO THE WAY GAVIN AND WAYNE JUST DID...
S. CARTER A. RYDER
© 1997.
27

YOU'VE SAID IT YOURSELF, BLOOD BITCH. BIG BITCH AND THOSE OTHER SCRAGS COULDN'T HAVE SURVIVED, NOBODY COULD HAVE!
I WANT TO BE SURE!
ANYWAY, I'M NOT GOING BACK UNTIL WE FIND OURSELVES A MAN OR TWO. TRIBE WON'T FUNCTION WITHOUT ONE AND YOU KNOW IT.
SO, IF THOSE SLAGS SURVIVED AND THEY STILL HAVE THAT MAN WITH THEM, THEN OUR PROBLEM'S SOLVED.
OTHERWISE, WE'RE GOING TO HAVE TO RAID SOME NEARBY TRIBE. THAT'S ALL THERE IS TO IT!
STILL WARM... NO MORE THAN TWO DAYS OLD. ...HAS TO BE THEM. MY GUESS IS THAT THEY'RE STILL ALIVE...
SO, WHICH WAY DID THEY GO, DARK BITCH?
TRACKS IN THE DIRT HERE ARE POINTING NORTH. IT FIGURES, TOO.
THAT'S THE WAY THAT GLOWING EMBER STREAKED ACROSS THE SKY A COUPLE OF NIGHTS BACK...
JUST LIKE THEM TO FOLLOW SOMETHING LIKE THAT. ESPECIALLY SINCE HARD BITCH IS WITH THEM,
SHE'S VERY KEEN WHEN IT COMES TO FOLLOWING OMENS.
S. CARTER ©'97

28

I'VE NEVER SEEN SUCH MASSIVE AND STRANGE BEASTS BEFORE, COLD BITCH!
THAT IS BECAUSE YOU'VE HARDLY EVER VENTURED FAR FROM THE TRIBE, PALE BITCH.
THOSE GIANT GRAZERS OUT THERE ARE SO FEARSOME THAT THEY SCARE OFF MOST OF THE MEAT-EATERS.
ALL OF THEM ARE ALIVE. OF THAT I'M CERTAIN. AND WE CAN'T BE MORE THAN TWO OR THREE DAYS BEHIND THEM.
GOOD! THIS TIME, WHEN WE CATCH THEM, WE'LL FINISH THEM! AND THAT MAN WILL BE COMING BACK WITH US!
AND YOU CAN TEACH HIM A LESSON NEVER TO RUN OFF AGAIN, DARK BITCH.
YEAH! I'D LIKE THAT!

CARTER
©
1997
29

84

JEZUZ AND JUDAS SHIT IN A BUCKET! THE LOCAL NATIVES ARE JUST AS HOSTILE AS THE FREAKY WILDLIFE!
THEY'RE NOT INTERESTED IN COMMUNICATING WITH US, THAT'S FOR SURE!
VYZT!
S.CARTER A.RYDYR ©1997

A GIFT HAS BEEN SENT TO US FROM THE DOMAIN OF THE GREAT GODDESS AKTUUK HERSELF!
THIS STRANGE EGG HAS HATCHED OPEN AND OUT HAVE COME TWO MEN!
THEN WHY DO THESE "GIFTS" RESIST SO? AND WITH SUCH MYSTERIOUS AND LETHAL, MAGIC WEAPONS!
ANSWER ME THAT!

IT'S A TEST OF OUR STRENGTH!
WE MUST PROVE WE ARE WORTHY OF THE GIFT!
DOK!
JEZUZ! POOR DAN!
QUESTION IS... IS HE DEAD?
OR DID IT JUST KNOCK HIM OUT?

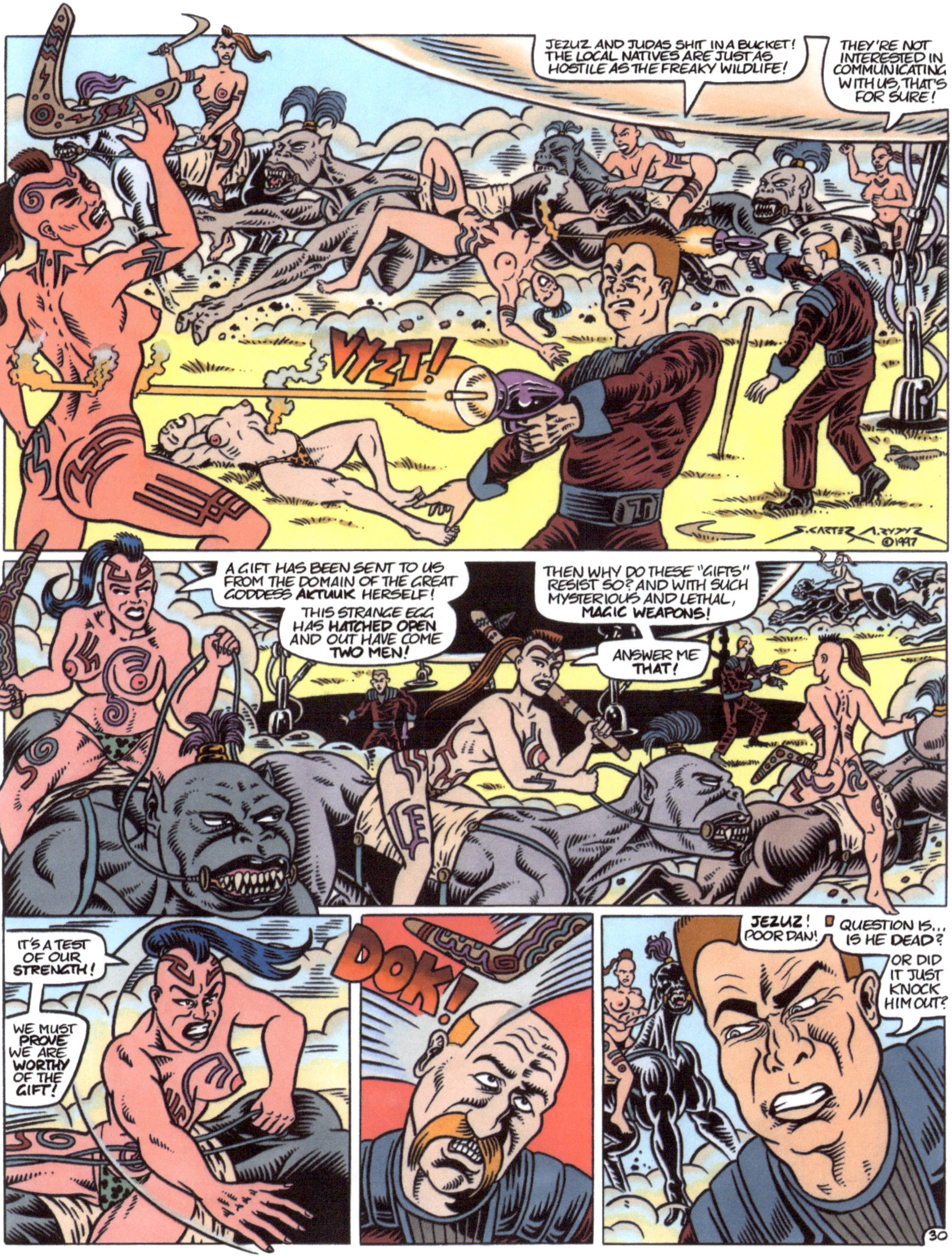

30

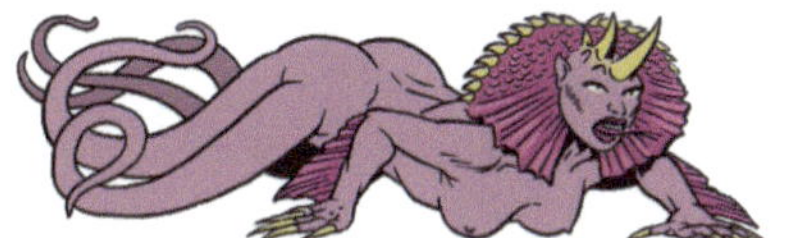

85

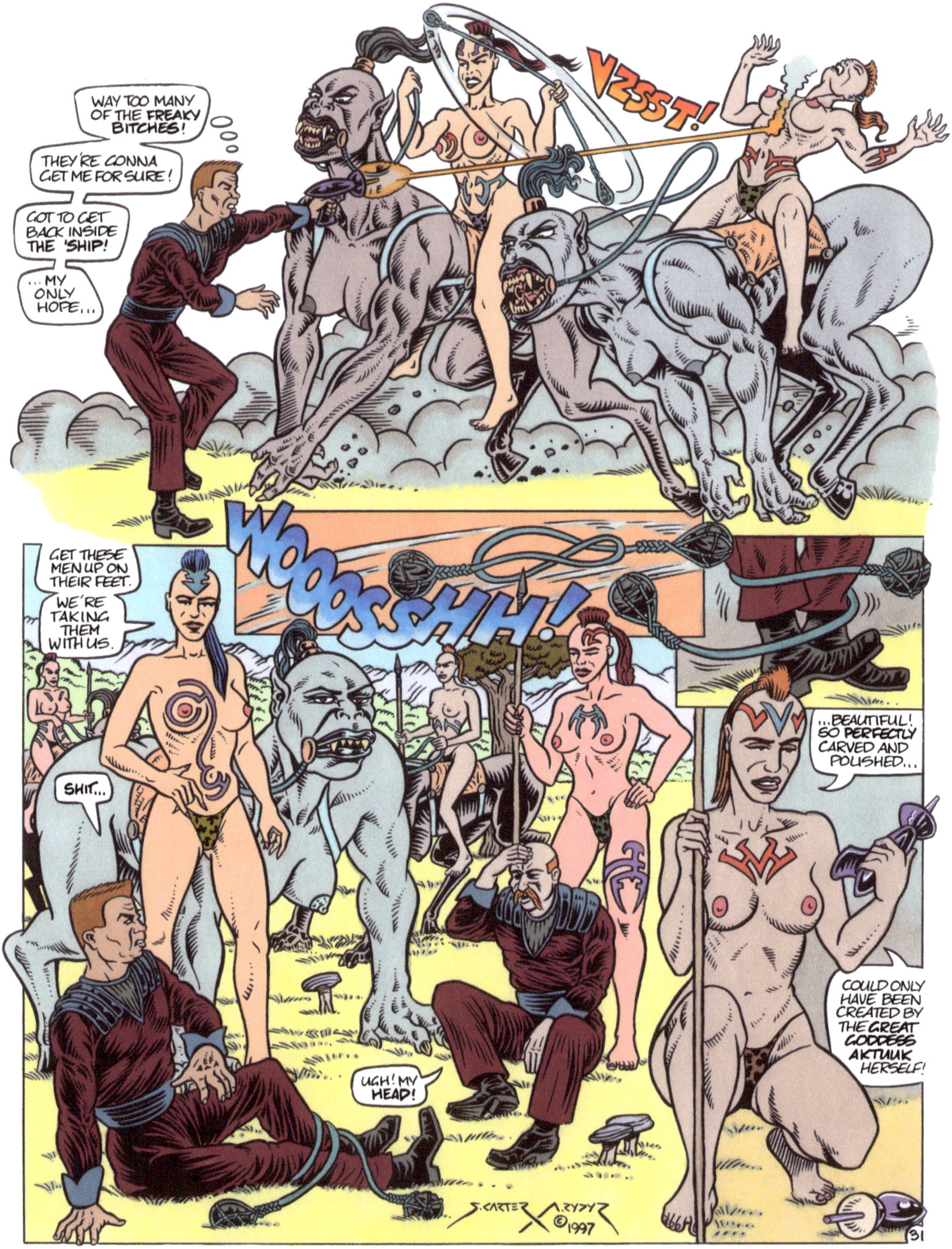

WAY TOO MANY OF THE FREAKY BITCHES!
THEY'RE GONNA GET ME FOR SURE!
GOT TO GET BACK INSIDE THE 'SHIP!
...MY ONLY HOPE...
VZSST!
GET THESE MEN UP ON THEIR FEET.
WE'RE TAKING THEM WITH US.
WOOOSSHH!
SHIT...
UGH! MY HEAD!
...BEAUTIFUL! SO PERFECTLY CARVED AND POLISHED...
COULD ONLY HAVE BEEN CREATED BY THE GREAT GODDESS AKTUUK HERSELF!
S.CARTER A.RYDYR ©1997
31

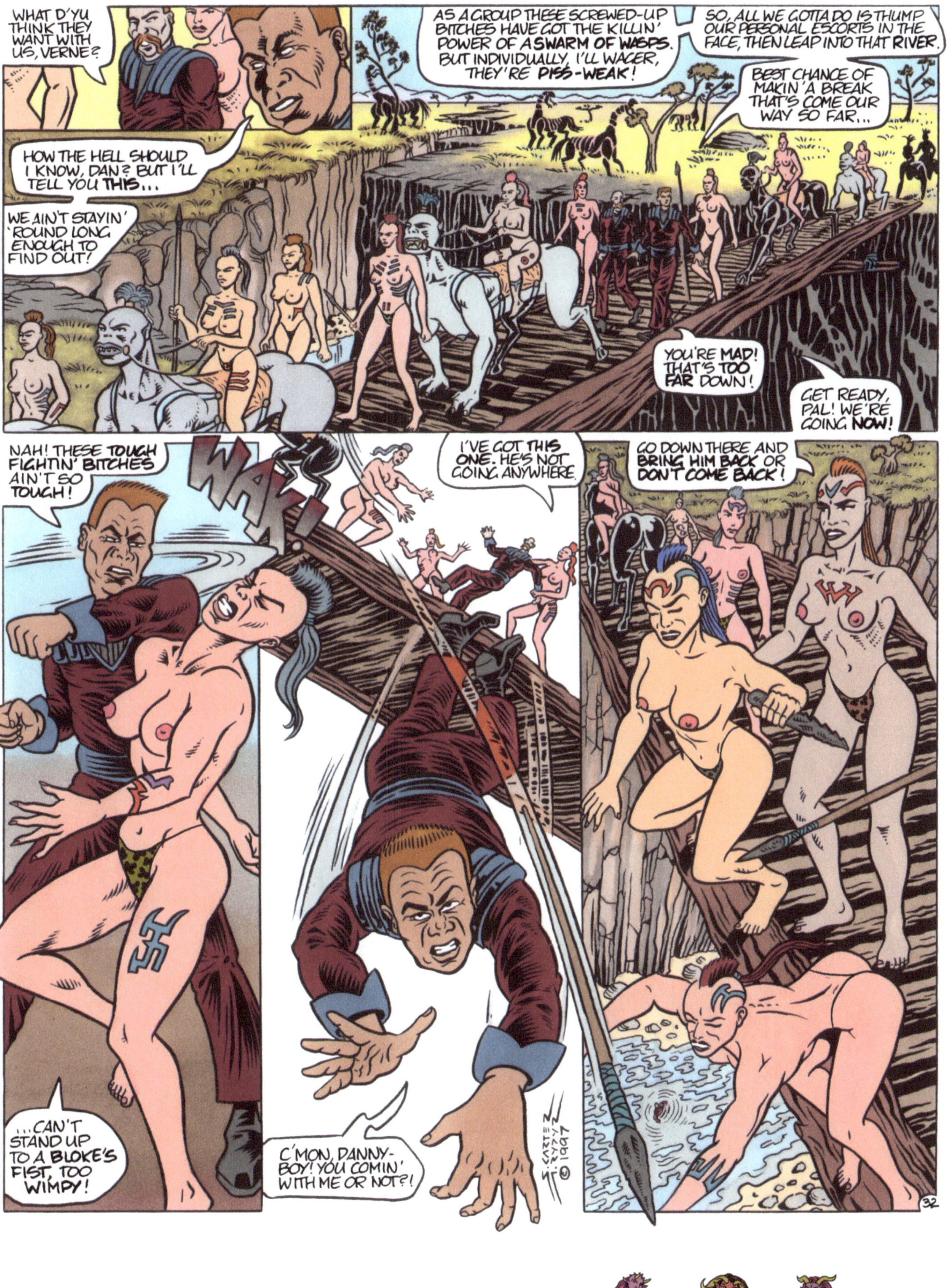

WHAT D'YU THINK THEY WANT WITH US, VERNE?
AS A GROUP THESE SCREWED-UP BITCHES HAVE GOT THE KILLIN' POWER OF A SWARM OF WASPS. BUT INDIVIDUALLY, I'LL WAGER, THEY'RE PISS-WEAK!
SO, ALL WE GOTTA DO IS THUMP OUR PERSONAL ESCORTS IN THE FACE, THEN LEAP INTO THAT RIVER.
BEST CHANCE OF MAKIN' A BREAK THAT'S COME OUR WAY SO FAR...
HOW THE HELL SHOULD I KNOW, DAN? BUT I'LL TELL YOU THIS...
WE AIN'T STAYIN' 'ROUND LONG ENOUGH TO FIND OUT!
YOU'RE MAD! THAT'S TOO FAR DOWN!
GET READY, PAL! WE'RE GOING NOW!
NAH! THESE TOUGH FIGHTIN' BITCHES AIN'T SO TOUGH!
WAK!
I'VE GOT THIS ONE. HE'S NOT GOING ANYWHERE.
GO DOWN THERE AND BRING HIM BACK OR DON'T COME BACK!
...CAN'T STAND UP TO A BLOKE'S FIST, TOO WIMPY!
C'MON, DANNY-BOY! YOU COMIN' WITH ME OR NOT?!

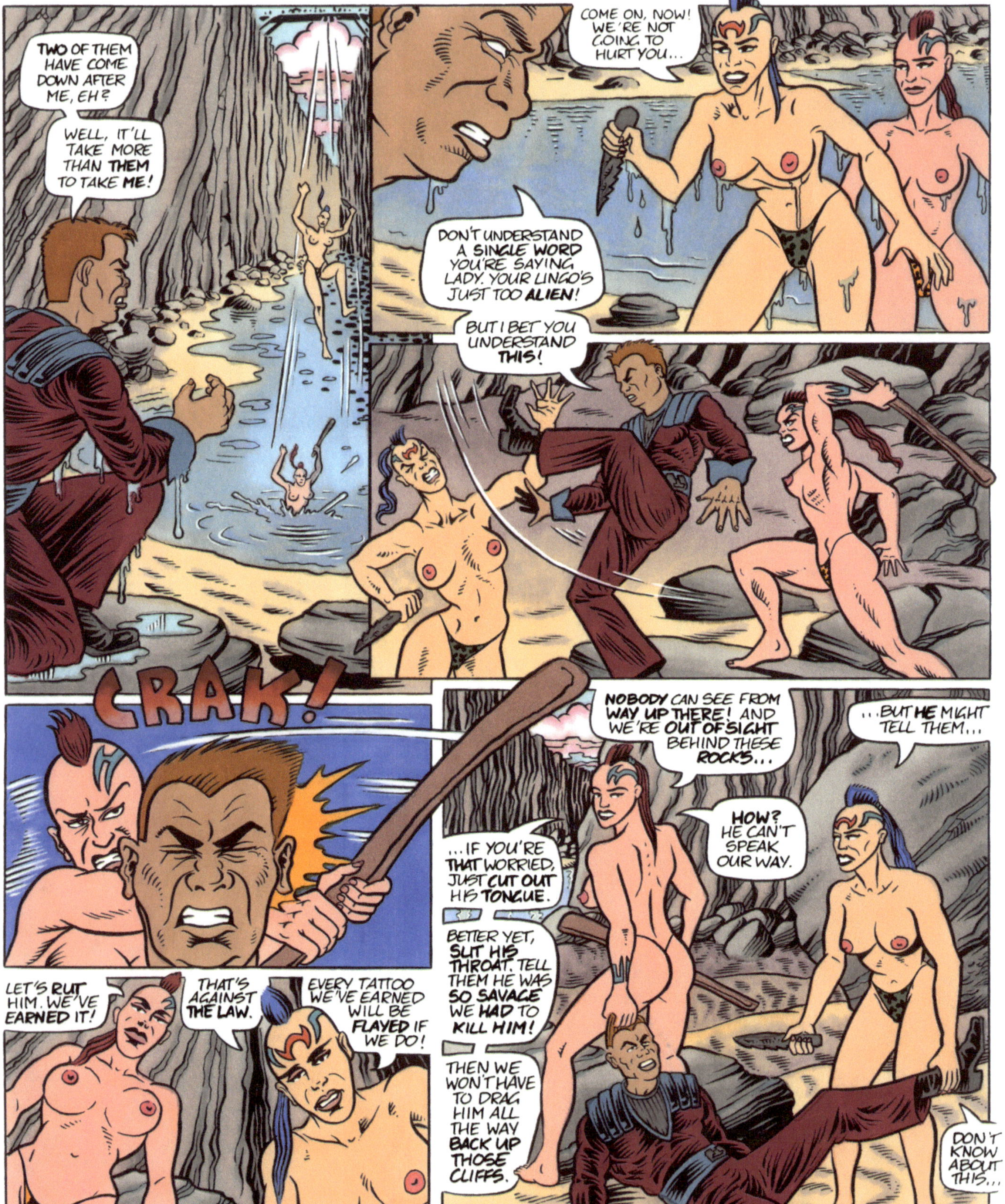

TWO OF THEM HAVE COME DOWN AFTER ME, EH?
WELL, IT'LL TAKE MORE THAN THEM TO TAKE ME!
COME ON, NOW! WE'RE NOT GOING TO HURT YOU...
DON'T UNDERSTAND A SINGLE WORD YOU'RE SAYING LADY. YOUR LINGO'S JUST TOO ALIEN!
BUT I BET YOU UNDERSTAND THIS!
CRAK!
NOBODY CAN SEE FROM WAY UP THERE! AND WE'RE OUT OF SIGHT BEHIND THESE ROCKS...
...BUT HE MIGHT TELL THEM...
HOW? HE CAN'T SPEAK OUR WAY.
...IF YOU'RE THAT WORRIED, JUST CUT OUT HIS TONGUE.
BETTER YET, SLIT HIS THROAT. TELL THEM HE WAS SO SAVAGE WE HAD TO KILL HIM!
THEN WE WON'T HAVE TO DRAG HIM ALL THE WAY BACK UP THOSE CLIFFS.
DON'T KNOW ABOUT THIS...
LET'S RUT HIM. WE'VE EARNED IT!
THAT'S AGAINST THE LAW.
EVERY TATTOO WE'VE EARNED WILL BE FLAYED IF WE DO!
S. CARTER A. RYYYR © 1997
33

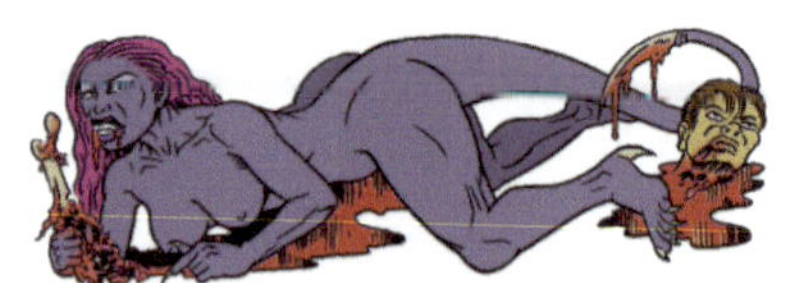

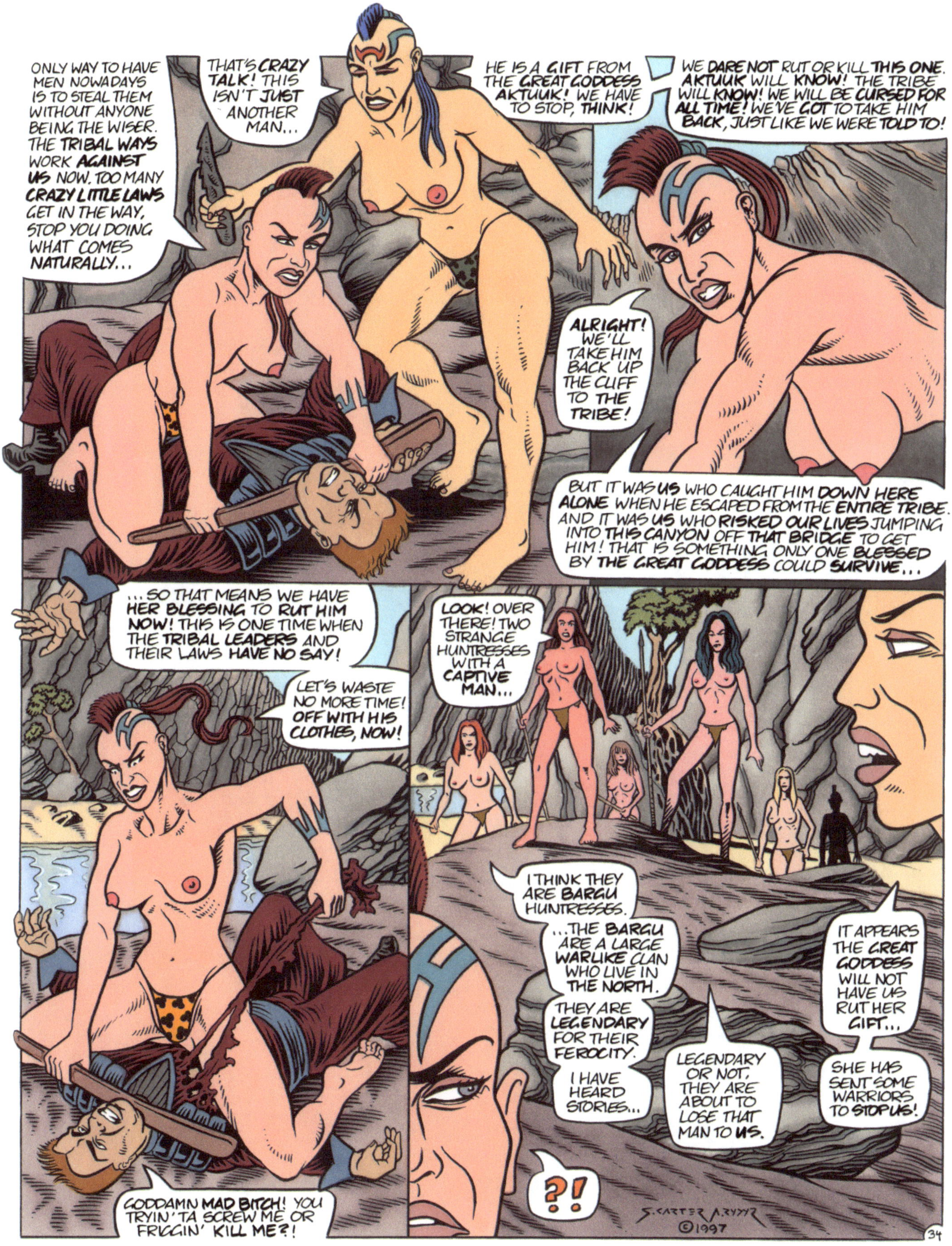

ONLY WAY TO HAVE MEN NOWADAYS IS TO STEAL THEM WITHOUT ANYONE BEING THE WISER. THE TRIBAL WAYS WORK AGAINST US NOW. TOO MANY CRAZY LITTLE LAWS GET IN THE WAY, STOP YOU DOING WHAT COMES NATURALLY...

THAT'S CRAZY TALK! THIS ISN'T JUST ANOTHER MAN...

HE IS A GIFT FROM THE GREAT GODDESS AKTUUK! WE HAVE TO STOP, THINK!

WE DARE NOT RUT OR KILL THIS ONE. AKTUUK WILL KNOW! THE TRIBE WILL KNOW! WE WILL BE CURSED FOR ALL TIME! WE'VE GOT TO TAKE HIM BACK, JUST LIKE WE WERE TOLD TO!

ALRIGHT! WE'LL TAKE HIM BACK UP THE CLIFF TO THE TRIBE!

BUT IT WAS US WHO CAUGHT HIM DOWN HERE ALONE WHEN HE ESCAPED FROM THE ENTIRE TRIBE. AND IT WAS US WHO RISKED OUR LIVES JUMPING INTO THIS CANYON OFF THAT BRIDGE TO GET HIM! THAT IS SOMETHING ONLY ONE BLESSED BY THE GREAT GODDESS COULD SURVIVE...

...SO THAT MEANS WE HAVE HER BLESSING TO RUT HIM NOW! THIS IS ONE TIME WHEN THE TRIBAL LEADERS AND THEIR LAWS HAVE NO SAY!

LET'S WASTE NO MORE TIME! OFF WITH HIS CLOTHES, NOW!

LOOK! OVER THERE! TWO STRANGE HUNTRESSES WITH A CAPTIVE MAN...

I THINK THEY ARE BARGU HUNTRESSES.

...THE BARGU ARE A LARGE WARLIKE CLAN WHO LIVE IN THE NORTH. THEY ARE LEGENDARY FOR THEIR FEROCITY.

I HAVE HEARD STORIES...

LEGENDARY OR NOT, THEY ARE ABOUT TO LOSE THAT MAN TO US.

IT APPEARS THE GREAT GODDESS WILL NOT HAVE US RUT HER GIFT...

SHE HAS SENT SOME WARRIORS TO STOP US!

GODDAMN MAD BITCH! YOU TRYIN' TA SCREW ME OR FRIGGIN' KILL ME?!

?!

S. CARTER ARYYR
©1997

34

GOTTA ADMIT, THESE BROADS 'R' PRETTY CUTE
... PITY THEY ALL SEEM TO BE MAD AS MEAT-AXES!
S. CARTER A. 1997
WHAT'S GOING ON DOWN THERE?
LOOKS LIKE THEY'VE RUN INTO TROUBLE WITH SOME TRIBESWOMEN.
?!
A SEA SNIPPER! WHAT IS ONE OF THOSE DOING SO FAR INLAND?!
THIS RIVER PROBABLY FLOWS OUT TO THE SEA, EVENTUALLY... THAT THING MUST HAVE VENTURED UPRIVER FROM THE DELTA AEONS AGO, FOUND ITSELF A DECENT SUPPLY OF GAME AND STAYED PUT...
IEEIK
35

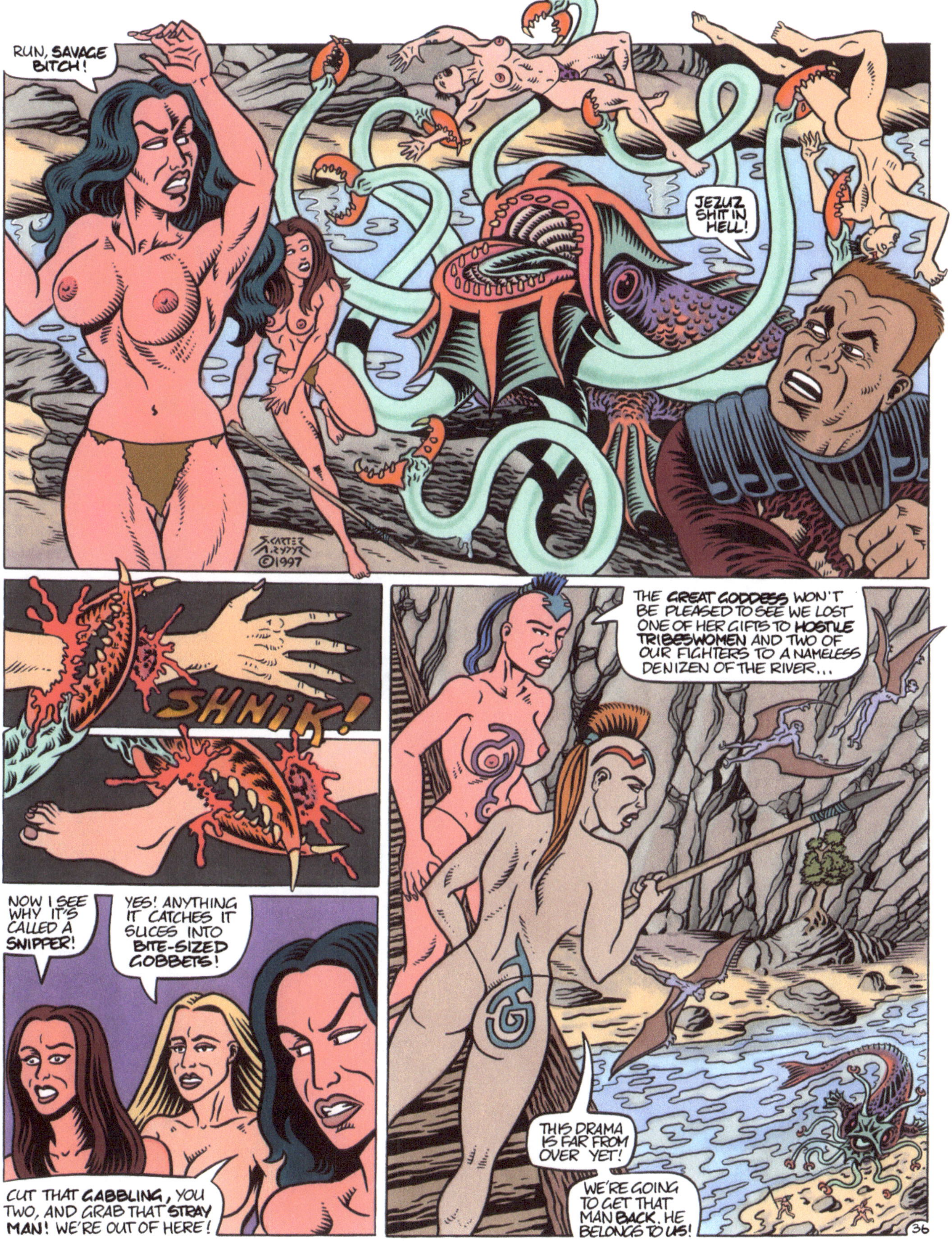

RUN, SAVAGE BITCH!
JEZUZ SHIT IN HELL!
SHNIK!
NOW I SEE WHY IT'S CALLED A SNIPPER!
YES! ANYTHING IT CATCHES IT SLICES INTO BITE-SIZED GOBBETS!
CUT THAT GABBLING, YOU TWO, AND GRAB THAT STRAY MAN! WE'RE OUT OF HERE!
THE GREAT GODDESS WON'T BE PLEASED TO SEE WE LOST ONE OF HER GIFTS TO HOSTILE TRIBESWOMEN AND TWO OF OUR FIGHTERS TO A NAMELESS DENIZEN OF THE RIVER...
THIS DRAMA IS FAR FROM OVER YET!
WE'RE GOING TO GET THAT MAN BACK. HE BELONGS TO US!

QUICK! THEY'RE GETTING AWAY!
GIVE ME ONE OF THOSE MAGIC WEAPONS THAT CAME WITH THOSE MEN. I'LL STOP THEM RIGHT NOW!
...THIS IS HOW THOSE MEN WERE HOLDING THEM!
BUT IT'S NOT WORKING! WHY?!
...BRING THAT MAN HERE, NOW!
YOU! SHOW ME WHAT LITTLE TRICK MAKES THIS THING WORK, RIGHT NOW!
CLIK! CLIK!
SILLY BITCH! SAFETY'S STILL ON, HEH! HEH!
WHAT IS HE BABBLING ABOUT?!
DON'T KNOW WHAT YER SAYIN', LADY. BUT I CAN SEE YOU WANT ME TO SHOW YOU HOW TO USE THAT WEAPON. ...WELL, TRUTH TO TELL, THERE'S NO WAY I'LL DO SOMETHING LIKE THAT!
CAN'T UNDERSTAND HIM. AND HE DOES NOT UNDERSTAND US. DOESN'T KNOW OUR LANGUAGE...
TAKE HIM BACK TO THE VILLAGE, ALONG WITH THOSE WEAPONS... IN THE MEANTIME, A SORTE OF US IS GOING TO HAVE TO GO DOWN INTO THAT CANYON AND TAKE BACK WHAT IS OURS...
THERE'S A PATHWAY DOWN THOSE CLIFFS A LITTLE FURTHER NORTHWARD. WE RIDE FAST ENOUGH, WE CAN GET AHEAD OF THEM AND CUT THEM OFF!
GOOD! LET'S MOVE!

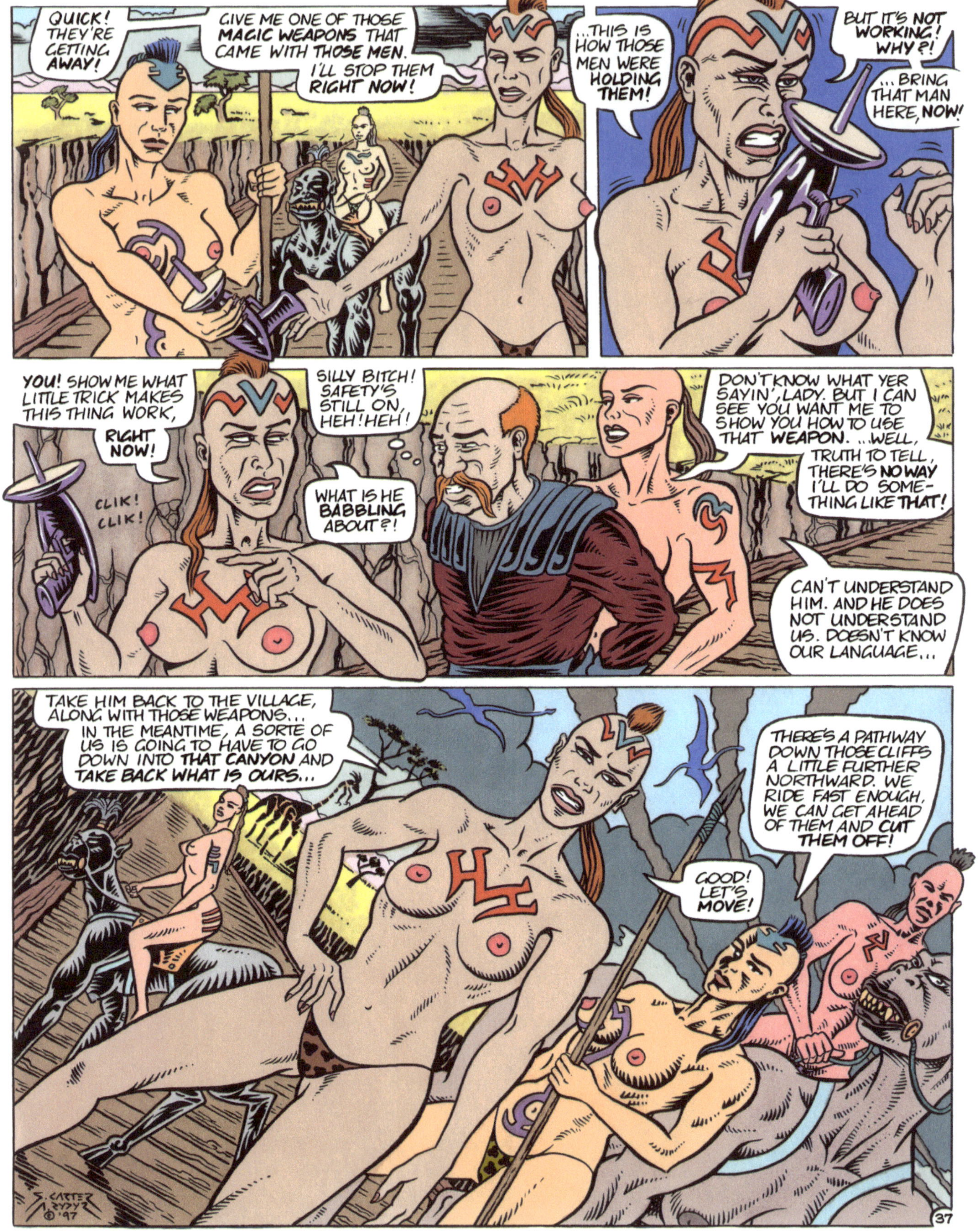

37

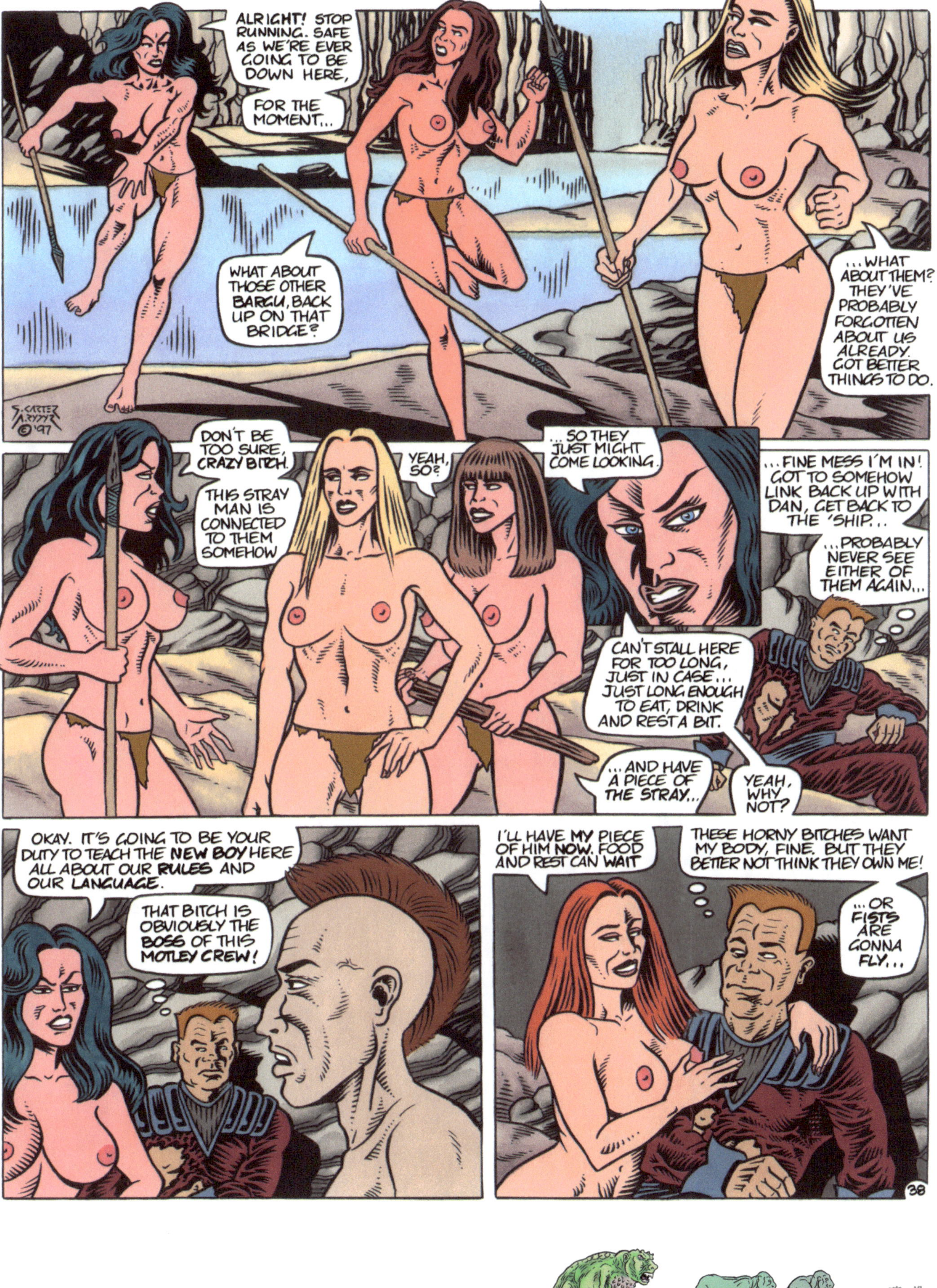

ALRIGHT! STOP RUNNING. SAFE AS WE'RE EVER GOING TO BE DOWN HERE,
FOR THE MOMENT...
WHAT ABOUT THOSE OTHER BARGU, BACK UP ON THAT BRIDGE?
...WHAT ABOUT THEM? THEY'VE PROBABLY FORGOTTEN ABOUT US ALREADY. GOT BETTER THINGS TO DO.
DON'T BE TOO SURE, CRAZY BITCH.
THIS STRAY MAN IS CONNECTED TO THEM SOMEHOW
YEAH, SO?
...SO THEY JUST MIGHT COME LOOKING.
...FINE MESS I'M IN! GOT TO SOMEHOW LINK BACK UP WITH DAN, GET BACK TO THE 'SHIP...
...PROBABLY NEVER SEE EITHER OF THEM AGAIN...
CAN'T STALL HERE FOR TOO LONG, JUST IN CASE... JUST LONG ENOUGH TO EAT, DRINK AND REST A BIT.
...AND HAVE A PIECE OF THE STRAY...
YEAH, WHY NOT?
OKAY. IT'S GOING TO BE YOUR DUTY TO TEACH THE NEW BOY HERE ALL ABOUT OUR RULES AND OUR LANGUAGE.
THAT BITCH IS OBVIOUSLY THE BOSS OF THIS MOTLEY CREW!
I'LL HAVE MY PIECE OF HIM NOW. FOOD AND REST CAN WAIT
THESE HORNY BITCHES WANT MY BODY, FINE. BUT THEY BETTER NOT THINK THEY OWN ME!
...OR FISTS ARE GONNA FLY...

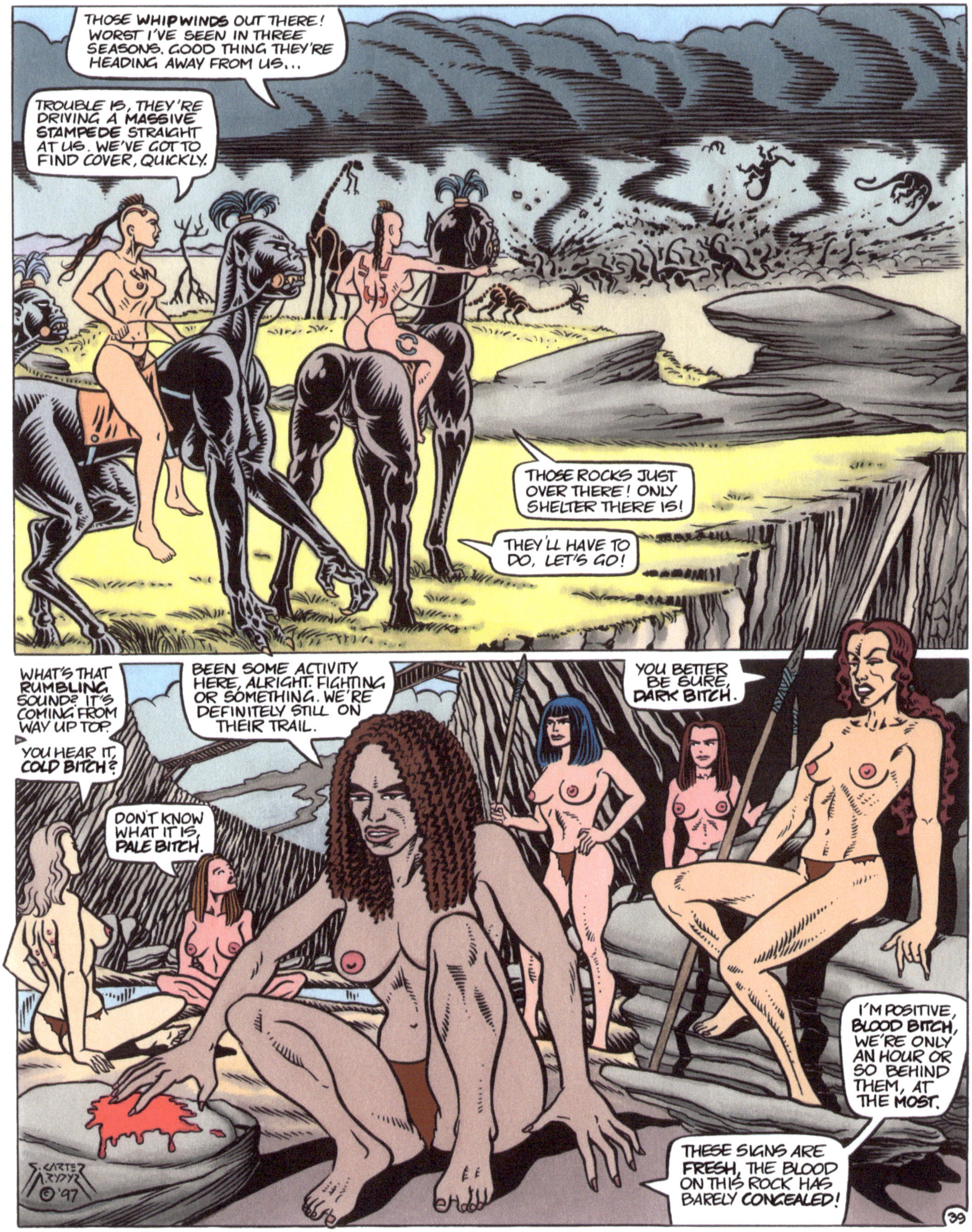

THOSE WHIP WINDS OUT THERE! WORST I'VE SEEN IN THREE SEASONS. GOOD THING THEY'RE HEADING AWAY FROM US...
TROUBLE IS, THEY'RE DRIVING A MASSIVE STAMPEDE STRAIGHT AT US. WE'VE GOT TO FIND COVER, QUICKLY.
THOSE ROCKS JUST OVER THERE! ONLY SHELTER THERE IS!
THEY'LL HAVE TO DO, LET'S GO!
WHAT'S THAT RUMBLING SOUND? IT'S COMING FROM WAY UP TOP. YOU HEAR IT, COLD BITCH?
BEEN SOME ACTIVITY HERE, ALRIGHT. FIGHTING OR SOMETHING. WE'RE DEFINITELY STILL ON THEIR TRAIL.
YOU BETTER BE SURE, DARK BITCH.
DON'T KNOW WHAT IT IS, PALE BITCH.
I'M POSITIVE, BLOOD BITCH, WE'RE ONLY AN HOUR OR SO BEHIND THEM, AT THE MOST.
THESE SIGNS ARE FRESH, THE BLOOD ON THIS ROCK HAS BARELY CONGEALED!

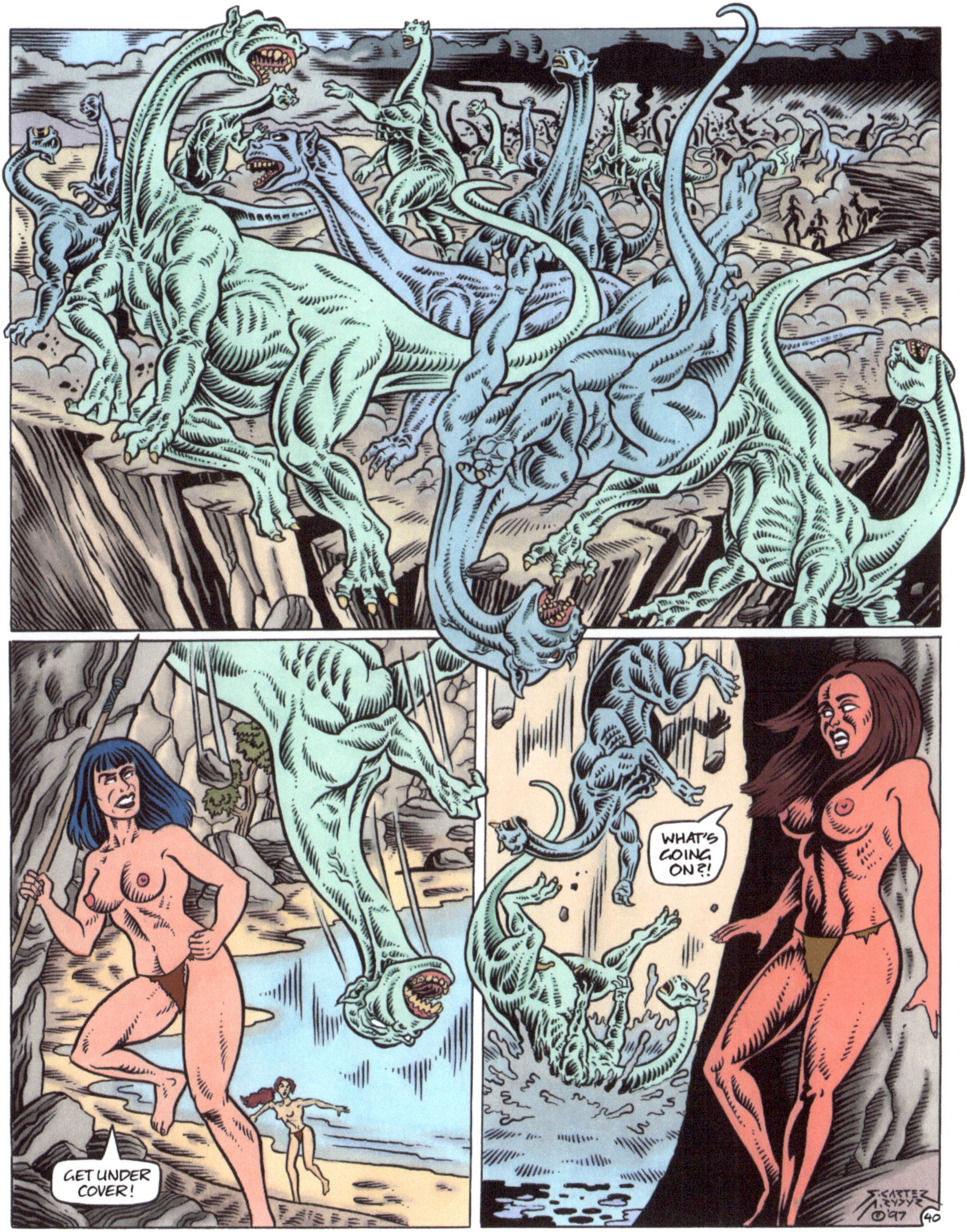

95

NEVER SEEN ANYTHING LIKE THIS! LUCKY IF I LIVE THROUGH IT!
THEY'RE STREWN RIGHT ACROSS THE PLAIN IN THE HUNDREDS! AND RUNNING OFF INTO THE CANYON IN A BLIND PANIC!
IT'S THE WRATH OF AKTUUK, THAT'S WHAT IT IS!
IT'S OVER, AT LAST.
AT LEAST HALF OF THAT HERD JUMPED INTO THE CANYON.
THE REST HAVE GONE BACK TO GRAZING LIKE IT NEVER EVEN HAPPENED...WEIRD!
ONLY US LEFT AND WE'VE LOST THE MAGIC WEAPONS AND THE MAN!
THE OTHERS WON'T BE PLEASED...
DON'T WORRY ABOUT THE OTHERS. THEY MIGHT NOT EVEN BE ALIVE AFTER ALL THIS. BEST WE GET BACK TO THE VILLAGE.
I SEE THAT THE CARRION HAGS ARE WASTING NO TIME PUTTING THEIR CLAIM ON ALL THAT DEAD MEAT...
CARTER RYYYY ©'97
41

WHAT INCREDIBLE CARNAGE...
...IF THERE'S SUCH A PLACE AS HELL, THEN THIS PLANET IS A CONTENDER WITH ITS DEADLY MENAGERIE OF GROTESQUE FREAKS.
IT'S A WONDER THIS IS STILL HERE. JUST AS WELL, COULDN'T GET BACK OVER TO THE 'SHIP OTHERWISE.
...HOPE IT'S STILL OKAY...
...GOT TO GET BACK, CLEAN UP, THEN COME BACK OUT HERE, TRY TO FIND VERNE...
YOU THINK THE OTHER PARTY SURVIVED THE STAMPEDE AND MANAGED TO GET BACK...?
ALL WE CAN DO IS HOPE THEY DID.
MEANWHILE, WE'RE STILL GOING DOWN THERE.
WE HAVE TO FIND THAT OTHER MAN...
© 1997
42

DON'T LIKE THIS. TOO MANY SCAVENGERS AND MEATEATERS.
THERE'S PLENTY FOR THEM TO EAT HERE. WE DON'T GET TOO CLOSE, THEY WON'T BOTHER US.
BLOOD CRESTED SQUABBLERS...
THEY FEROCIOUSLY DEFEND THEIR MEAT. DON'T DO ANYTHING TO SET THEM OFF!
NEVER FELT MORE NAKED WITHOUT A GUN.
...OH, NO! THIS IS ALL WE NEED!
AND WHAT HAVE WE HERE? IT'S THE SCRAG BUNCH!
THIS TIME WE FINISH IT!
S. CARTER ARYYR © '97
43

WHAT A WHACKO PLANET! FULL OF MUTANT FREAKS AND HOPPING-MAD BITCHES!
NO DOUBT VIOLENCE IS MORE ORGASMIC TO THEM THAN SEX!
EEYAG!
WAK!
SWOOSH
SK' RARK!
THAT'S DONE IT NOW!
SKRAK!
PLACE'S SWARMING WITH THEM!
SCAZ © '91
44

99

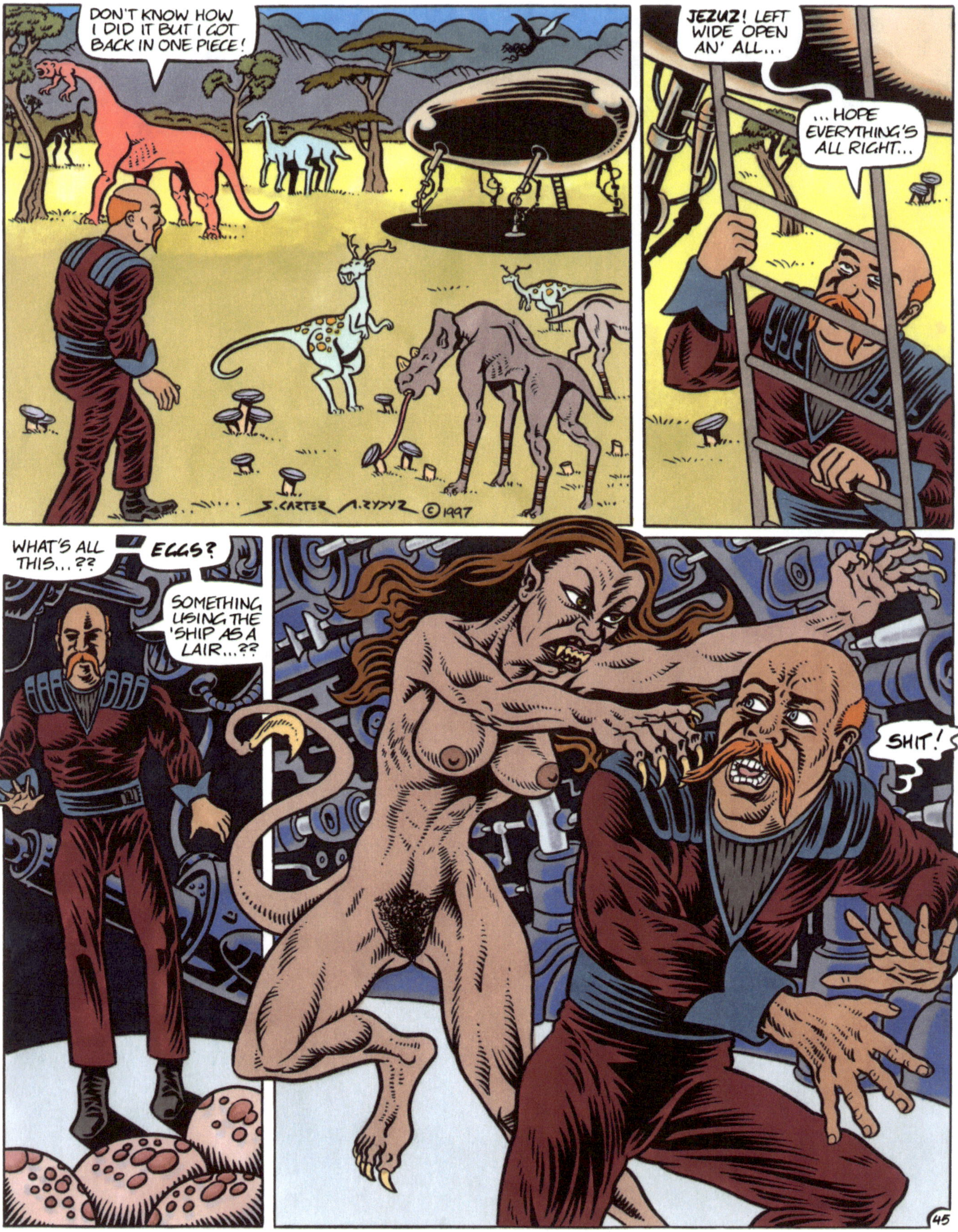

DON'T KNOW HOW I DID IT BUT I GOT BACK IN ONE PIECE!
S.CARTER A.ZYDYZ © 1997
JEZUZ! LEFT WIDE OPEN AN' ALL...
...HOPE EVERYTHING'S ALL RIGHT...
WHAT'S ALL THIS...??
EGGS?
SOMETHING USING THE 'SHIP AS A LAIR...??
SHIT!
45

ONLY WAY OUT IS UP.
MOVE IT, SAVAGE BITCH!
STAY IN HERE... ONLY ONE ENTRANCE, EASIER TO FIGHT THEM OFF.
NOW THEY'RE ATTACKING ONE ANOTHER!
THEY'VE GONE CRAZY!
THEIR AGGRESSION'S SPREADING LIKE A GRASS FIRE, RAGING OUT OF CONTROL!

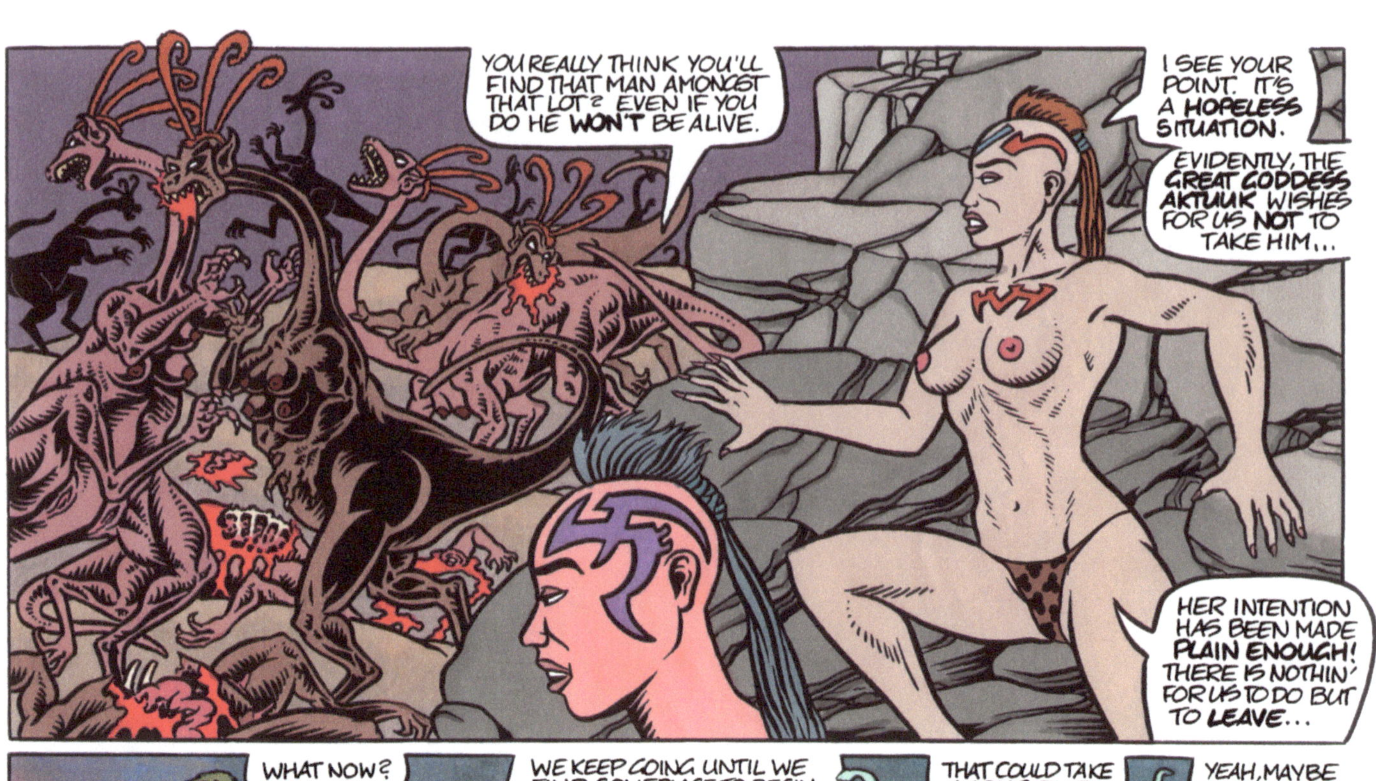

YOU REALLY THINK YOU'LL FIND THAT MAN AMONGST THAT LOT? EVEN IF YOU DO HE WON'T BE ALIVE.
I SEE YOUR POINT. IT'S A HOPELESS SITUATION.
EVIDENTLY, THE GREAT GODDESS AKTUUK WISHES FOR US NOT TO TAKE HIM...
HER INTENTION HAS BEEN MADE PLAIN ENOUGH! THERE IS NOTHIN' FOR US TO DO BUT TO LEAVE...
WHAT NOW?
WE KEEP GOING UNTIL WE FIND SOMEPLACE TO BEGIN A NEW LIFE AND A NEW TRIBE.
THAT COULD TAKE A LONG TIME.
YEAH, MAYBE A LIFETIME.
I'M HUNGRY AND TIRED.
S. CARTER
© 1997
47

SCAZ
2012-13

sCR 2013

If you enjoyed this book by *SCAR*, have a look at their other titles and please consider writing a review. Thanks!

WEIRD WILD WEST

A New Novel by Carter Rydyr & Ethan Somerville

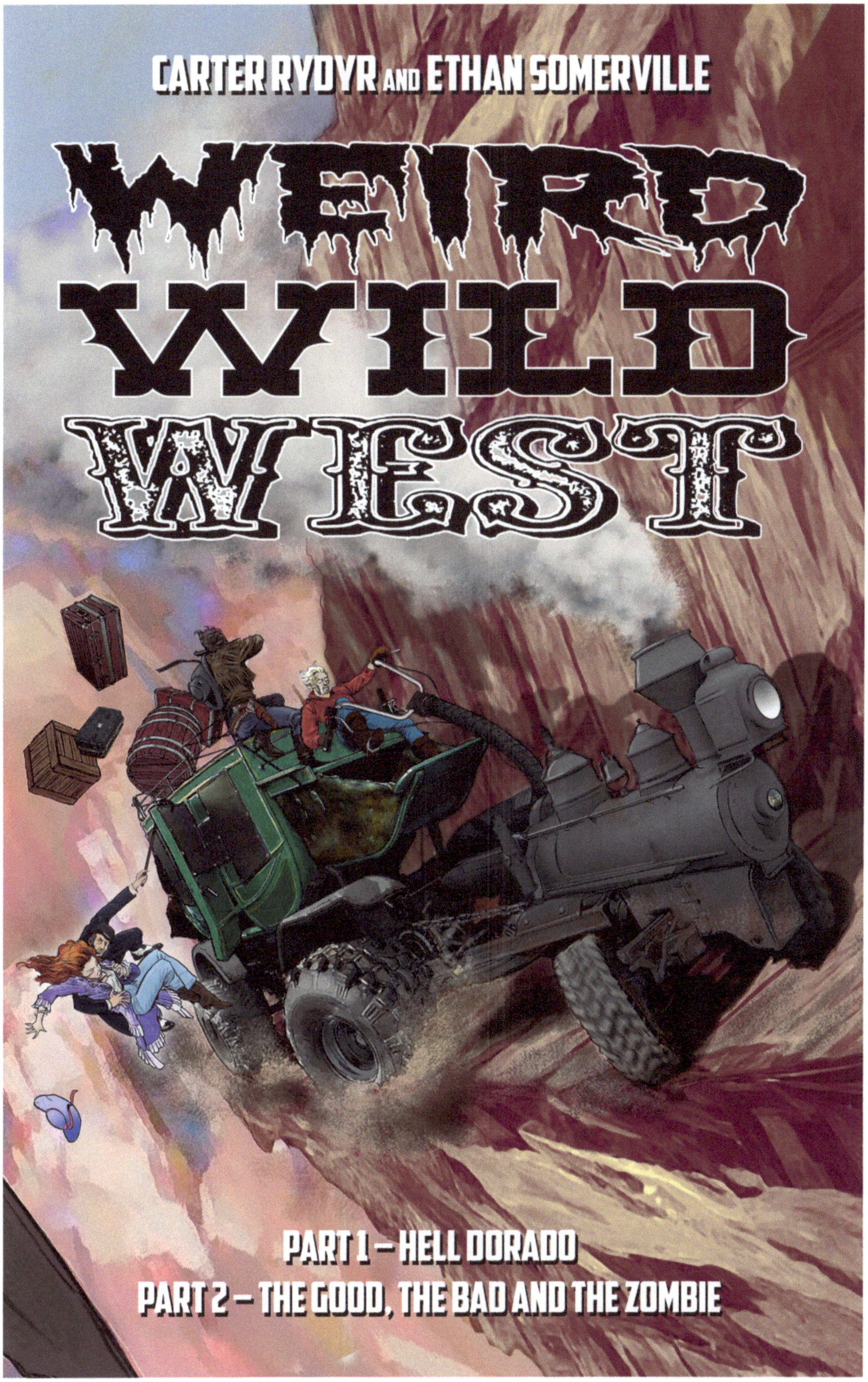

CARTER RYDYR AND ETHAN SOMERVILLE

WEIRD WILD WEST

PART 1 – HELL DORADO

PART 2 – THE GOOD, THE BAD AND THE ZOMBIE

Imagine a wild west that isn't just full of cowboys and outlaws, saloon girls and gamblers. Imagine a wild west that isn't just cacti, tumbleweeds and rolling desert as far as the eye can see. Imagine a wild west of mechanical horses, mutant killer plants, flying dinosaurs, headless indians and fearsome zombie gunslingers hell-bent on revenge.

Imagine the Weird Wild West.

Six colourful characters, some not entirely human, embark on a perilous journey south from Sunbleached Plains to Kellyville. A dapper dentist, a southern belle, a wealthy madam, a retired banker turned gambler, an orphaned boy and a travelling body-parts salesman all trade their various stories to pass the time.

Driving the carriage is one Zeke "the Freak" Sarandon, a retired soldier with more than one strange, nervous habit. Although he is an experienced traveller, and the only one insane enough to take the most direct route south, even he cannot prevent his passengers from each meeting their grisly demise, one by one.

Hot on the trail of the coach, astride an ancient mechanical horse blowing sparks and belching out toxic clouds of smoke, is a zombie gunslinger, the risen corpse of a murdered prospector.

For on the carriage is the one who killed him, and he must have his horrible, bloody revenge.

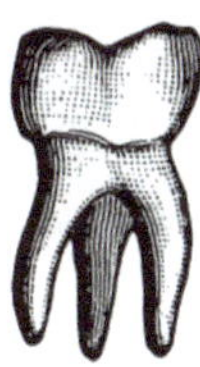

Bizarro Pulp Press

an imprint of JournalStone Publishing.

Published 2018

ISBN: 978-1-947654-40-2

MORE BOOKS BY S.C.A.R.

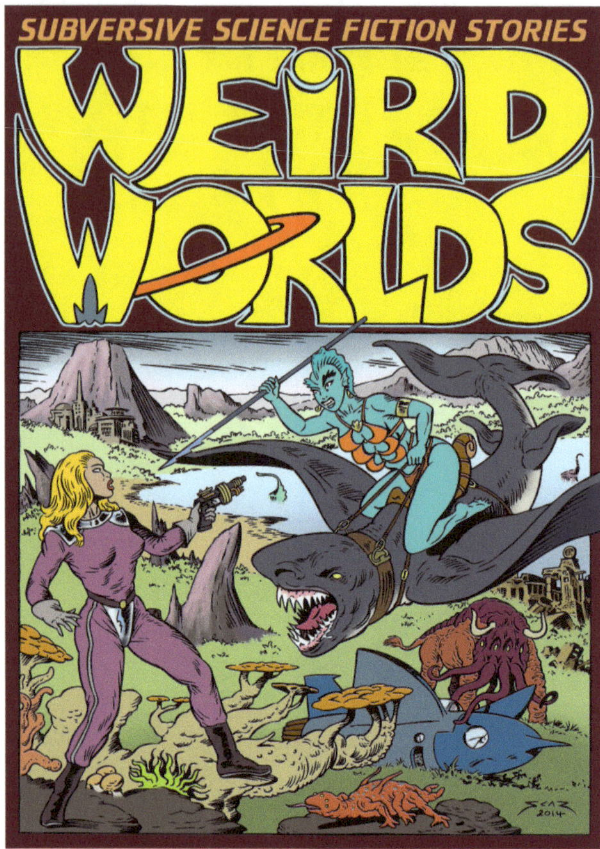

Savage Bitch: ISBN 978-0987622907
Phantastique: ISBN 978-0987622938

Weird Worlds: ISBN 978-0987622914
Fantastique: ISBN 978-0987622921

www.weirdwildart.com

MORE BOOKS BY S.C.A.R.

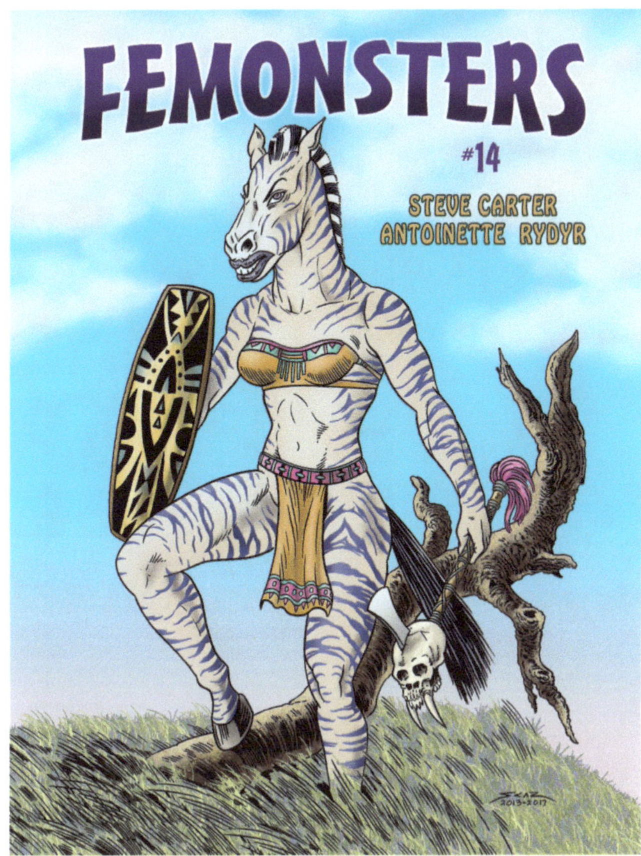

Femonsters #14: ISBN 978-0987622969
Bestiary of Monstruum: ISBN 978-0987622945

New World Disorder: ISBN 978-0987622976
Weird Sex Fantasy: ISBN 978-0987622952

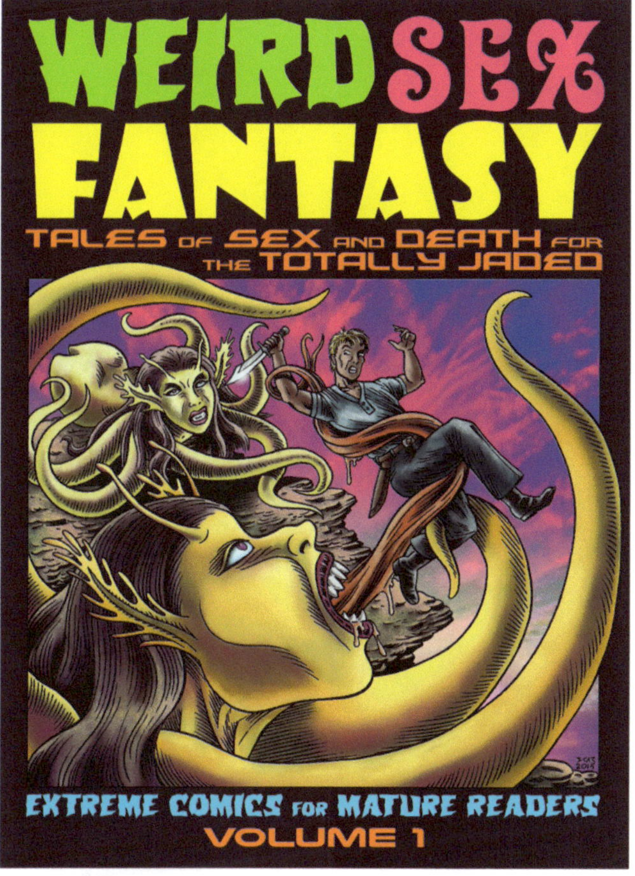

www.weirdwildart.com

www.ingramcontent.com/pod-product-compliance
Lightning Source LLC
Chambersburg PA
CBHW042138120726
47911CB00022B/116